OF
SUN
AND
RUBY

THE WEATHER COURT GEM SERIES

KC SILVER

Copyright © 2026 by KC Silver

All rights reserved.

No portion of this book may be reproduced in any form without written permission from the publisher or author, except as permitted by U.S. copyright law.

To those still learning who they want to be: let your light shine bright in all the different versions of yourself.

One

This court has too many windows, Iskra thought to herself as she wiped the glass. With the sun glaring through it, the stubborn smudges never seemed to disappear. It was as if they were trapped here, just like her. Could this be all life had to offer? A dirty rag, sweat trickling down her brows?

Then, the music and cheers roared behind her, a reminder there was more out there to explore. Iskra did not know the reason behind such a celebration, but she longingly dreamed of standing with the crowd, a ribbon in her hand as she danced. Her feet would ache, her breath would become labored, but she would be living. She would be *free*. Once upon a time, she had the ability to wander without a phantom chain around her throat, but Kryth held her tight now.

"I never said to stop," Kryth reprimanded as he exited his shop and stood on the small stoop, his brown eyes focused on the crowd.

She considered mouthing back but stopped herself. The one time she yelled at Kryth for pushing her around, she was rewarded with not being let out of her cage for a week. Her time was already limited, so she refused to let her attitude cut it shorter.

3

Iskra kept quiet, returning to cleaning the shop's windows, the same mundane task she did every week for her owner. She had the mark on the right side of her ribs claiming her as his, the curse he'd stamped onto her skin right after he caught her.

Kryth lit his pipe, inhaling a puff. She watched the smoke leave his mouth as he exhaled, white slithering into the air like a dragon in flight.

"That'll kill you," Iskra said as she knelt to clean a lower corner. She didn't dare let her eyes wander to the inside of the shop, where the usually shut opaque curtains were wide open. Beyond Kryth's apothecary—used as a front to hide his true identity—countless cages hung from the ceiling, and the vacant one caused her body to tighten. A brazen move from Kryth, but perhaps he assumed anyone would be too drunk to even notice the dragons squirming in their cages, desperate for an escape. Iskra couldn't stomach the sight of the other trapped shifters, knowing one day, they would have a fate just like hers.

"Goddess Slone has shown me I'll be okay," Kryth's voice brought her back to the present, outside in the sun, where her limbs were human.

"Perhaps the Goddess of Sun only shows you what you want to see," Iskra mumbled.

"What's that?" he asked, but she didn't have a chance to respond before they were interrupted by laughing that grew louder with each passing second.

Iskra turned toward the noise, finding two figures bounding toward the shop. One was skipping ahead, the other chasing after them. Both of them wore cloaks made of velvet, one red, the other a deep blue. She imagined they were drenched underneath, with the sun at its peak. Their hoods were up and their heads ducked, so Iskra couldn't get a look at their faces. Kryth seemed curious as he approached Iskra's side, taking another puff from his pipe. She swiped at the smoke, gagging at the smell.

The strangers' identities remained hidden as they got closer. Though that was quickly fixed as one of the figures tripped and fell. At first, Iskra looked for a rock or a crack in the street, but it was Kryth's foot stretched out instead.

"Lady Esi," a male voice called out, running after his fallen friend. He bent to cover the woman, but it was too late. Iskra and Kryth saw the woman's long, black hair, the waves smooth and shiny. Iskra instinctively went to brush her fingers through her own matted auburn tresses, but her digits caught in tangles.

As the woman stood and her profile was revealed, Iskra stopped what she was doing, the blood draining from her face. She could feel Kryth stiffen next to her.

"Stop worrying so much, Bron," the beautiful woman brushed off his help. She unbuttoned the cloak, slipping it off, and Iskra was assaulted by the scent of clove and orange. "I know you're trying to protect me, but it's much too hot for this."

The woman still had not turned her focus to Iskra and Kryth, but Bron had noticed, his porcelain face ashening to an even lighter tone.

"Lady Esi..." Bron reached out, grabbing the cloak from the ground. "I think we should go."

"Don't be ridiculous. I'm sure these are nice strangers." Esi finally directed her attention to Iskra, and she almost stumbled and fell again. "*Oh.*"

Iskra and Esi were only arm lengths apart, and it felt like Iskra was looking in a mirror. They had the same amber eyes, the same freckles along their cheeks, the same tan skin. Only the color of their hair separated them, along with the state of their clothes: Iskra's plain dress was dusty while Esi's silk gown sheened in the sun.

Esi reached out her hand, as if to touch Iskra, but Kryth yanked Iskra away.

"Who are you?" Kryth's voice was vicious and cold.

Esi shook her head. The shock must have worn off as her mouth inched toward a mischievous smile. "I think you're the answer to my prayers."

They huddled in the front room of Kryth's shop only after he had a chance to shut the curtains.

With only two chairs at a small table in the corner Kryth usually used for appointments with patients, Iskra allowed Esi and Kryth to sit while she and Bron remained standing. Bron seemed uncomfortable as he stationed himself behind Esi. It gave Iskra the impression of a dragon guarding a great treasure, but the truth of their relationship was soon to be revealed, Iskra felt.

Iskra backed toward the wall to give herself space, but, in doing so, she hit her head on a shelf. Glasses rattled, and Iskra jolted forward before one of the vials of powder shattered on the stone floor. Since Kryth had shut the window curtains to avoid prying eyes, it was dark in the room, and just the thought of having to clean shards of glass in here sounded horrifying. Kryth glared at her, and she tightened her lips as she put the vial back in its place.

Clearing his throat, Kryth started, "What exactly may I do for you?"

"Not you," Esi quipped and pointed at Iskra. "Her."

"Whatever involves her involves me," Kryth snapped.

Esi narrowed her eyes, assessing the man before her. "Are you her father?"

Iskra coughed into her hand, trying to hide her laugh. Kryth was only a few years older than her—at least, that was what he claimed—but one couldn't tell from his appearance. His hair was currently gray, his brown eyes had crinkles around them, and his hands were wrinkled with sunspots. He had purposefully aged himself to play the role of this shop's owner. She knew when he played the minister, he turned the gray silver, the brown eyes glacier blue, and his skin stretched back to a youthful glow.

"My relationship to her is not your concern." Kryth crossed his arms, leaning back in the chair. He was growing more exasperated with every passing second of this conversation.

Iskra's eyes bounced between them, curious to hear this important woman's plan for her.

"Perhaps we should start with who exactly she is," Bron said from his spot on the opposite wall from Iskra. "How in the gods' names do you look identical to Esi?"

"Except for the hair." Esi twirled the ends of hers. "Mine is much prettier."

Iskra looked to Kryth for guidance. He grunted, waving away the question. "I have no idea. Perhaps she is a bastard daughter of one of your parents. Perhaps the gods like to toy with us for fun. I do not care. I do, however, care for why you want to use her."

"Right." Esi crossed her hands on the table, poised and proper, ready to state her case. "I'm Lady Esi, and this is my guard, Bron." She gestured to the stoic man behind her. "I'm from the northern region of the Sun Court, and I'm to be wedded to Prince Jasyn."

"The Sun Court Prince," Kryth said through his teeth.

"The one and only, now that the eldest son is dead."

"Why would they marry him off before he has proved himself in the Undertaking?"

"To restore confidence," Esi explained. "The royals have a singular heir left before their legacy is ruined. If Jasyn fails—if he doesn't get the Heart or dies—their line will die out. King Aleks is no longer able to compete after last year's Undertaking left him in a wheelchair."

"Then I ask again: what does Iskra have to do with any of this?"

Esi sighed, looking into her lap. "I have only a few weeks left of freedom before our marriage. I want to spend it with...someone who means something to me. I can't do that if I'm stuck in that glass castle."

Two

The asymmetrical, slate stone floors bit into Jasyn's feet as he jogged down the long hall. His hands fumbled with the buttons of his shirt. His morning in the sun left him no time to get properly dressed, and he knew it was going to displease his parents. After all, he was minutes away from meeting his future wife.

"Sometimes, I dread the day I'll have to call you king," Mych's teasing voice echoed from his station at the door.

Jasyn slowed, his breathing evening out with each step.

"Are they in there?"

Mych smiled, his crooked teeth showing. It made the brass armor and sword at his hip less intimidating, though Mych had never been able to embody what was expected from a guard. He was too soft-hearted and flirtatious for that. It was the reason he was the only person Jasyn talked to outside the royal family. Well...only his parents now. Both his older brother and sister were dead—Jaymes and Dahlia were only memories, ones he held tightly.

"Everyone is waiting for you," Mych said as he stepped up to Jasyn, fixing the buttons Jasyn hadn't lined up properly in his rush. Jasyn's face heated at his disheveled appearance.

Once Mych made Jasyn look somewhat presentable, Jasyn rolled his sore shoulders back and opened the door before he had anyone waiting any longer. It was embarrassing enough that he was late.

Mych patted him on the shoulder, a gesture of comfort as all eyes turned toward Jasyn.

Sunlight gilded the room, blinding until Jasyn blinked. Each corner was covered in greenery; in order to reach the dais where his parents sat on their thrones, he had to walk on stepping stones through a rectangular pond, where the water sprouted lily pads floating on top.

His parents gave him a reproachful glare as he reached them. They were both dressed in their best finery. His mother's long yellow dress accentuated her dark skin, and gold jewelry oozed off her neck, ears, and wrists. His father, seated on his throne instead of in his wheelchair, wore freshly pressed slacks and a purple shirt he favored for important occasions. Of all the royal children, Jasyn and his father looked the most similar, from their golden brown skin to their green eyes.

Both his parents had crowns planted on their heads.

"Were shoes too difficult to find?" were his mother's first words to him.

Jasyn's face flamed even hotter. He peered down at his bare feet, and his father chuckled.

"Let's hope your betrothed doesn't mind someone who spends more time with plants than people," his father joked.

Jasyn grunted, but he climbed up the few steps and bent to give his mother a kiss on the cheek.

"If she even likes me enough to stay," Jasyn cautioned.

"Of course she will, Jasyn. But you must get in your place so she can actually meet you," his mother said.

"Right," he said under his breath as he took the seat on his father's left side. It still felt strange to occupy this spot when it should have been Jaymes or Dahlia here. They were meant to rule, but they had sacrificed themselves for their dynasty and failed. Would Jasyn be next?

Jasyn peeked behind him to where his father's wheelchair was situated. A guard must have carried his father onto the throne. No matter how much Jasyn and his mother urged the king to replace the throne so he could just sit in his wheelchair. After all, they had built a ramp so he could wheel up easily, yet his father wouldn't listen. King Aleks had countered that he only had a short time left until Jasyn took his spot. Jasyn appreciated the faith, but he didn't think it was earned.

A wind chime jingled from outside, and before Jasyn had another moment to prepare, the door opened.

"Lady Esi," Mych announced, sending Jasyn a wink before he backed up a step.

Jasyn narrowed his eyes, but they quickly widened again as Lady Esi walked through the glass doors. Her eyes roamed the room, her neck craning upwards, taking in the scenery. It was called a glass castle for a reason. All the external walls were panes of glass, supported by the same ivory stone of the floors. Yet, it was like the windows didn't exist because the foliage outside bled inside. One could even still hear the elements like birds chirping and the swaying of leaves as the wind gusted.

"Lady Esi," his father said, and she seemed to come out of a trance as she finally settled her gaze on the dais, directly on *him*. He could have sworn he saw flames in those amber eyes. "And Mr. Bron," his father greeted with a dip of his head.

He had been so distracted by the glowing beauty of Lady Esi, the rich burgundy color of her chiffon dress and the way it accentuated her dark hair, he didn't notice her guard behind her. Unlike her, he appeared unimpressed with his surroundings. Like any competent guard, his attention was solely on the woman he was sworn to protect.

Esi's steps were awkward across the pond, but she held her head high, and Jasyn had to admire that bravery.

"King Aleks and Queen Kait, pleasure to meet you," she curtsied. Her voice was light with a slight rasp, like she was attempting to sound approachable, and it only enticed him further. He was on the edge of his seat as she nodded at him. "Prince Jasyn."

His mother stood and walked down the few steps to be level with Esi. Jasyn didn't fail to notice Bron's hand moving toward the hilt of his sword, how the guards around the perimeter mirrored Bron's movement. Clearly, Bron wasn't enthused about this betrothal.

"Thank you for traveling to meet my son." Queen Kait softly smiled, her dark, coiled curls framing her face.

"It is my honor." Esi bowed her head, her long hair slipping over her shoulders.

His mother turned to Jasyn, and she jerked her chin, gesturing for him to move. "I'm sure you have been anxiously waiting to meet my son."

Jasyn stumbled off the dais, and he heard his father snort under his breath.

"It is a pleasure." Jasyn extended his hand to Esi. She stood there blinking, hesitating, making him look like a fool. Her guard cleared his throat, and when she finally seemed to realize her gaffe, she gave Jasyn her hand. He took it, pressing a soft kiss to the back. Sparks danced wherever their skin touched. He couldn't help but linger, taking in her clove and orange scent. It was intoxicating.

A small gasp came from her lips, and he knew she felt it too. He didn't expect there to be such an immediate connection, but he felt something shift in him already. It was a scary revelation that someone had such power over his desire so quickly.

"I can tell this is a match straight from The Weather Gods," his mother said jovially, clapping her hands together in delight as she turned toward his father.

"I hope you aren't disappointed."

Jasyn didn't register Esi's words at first, but then he was shaking his head, almost disturbed by the idea of such a negative thought.

"Never. I am delighted to know once I complete the Undertaking, I will have you by my side."

"You don't even know me." She shrugged.

"We'll make sure to fix that," Jasyn responded. It would be a test almost as difficult as the Undertaking itself. Would he be able to open up to someone? It had been so long since he'd allowed himself to.

"I look forward to it." Esi smiled, her countenance brighter than the sun itself.

As soon as Iskra was in the privacy of her designated room, she slumped her shoulders and kicked off the heels Esi had given her. That introduction had not been what she had expected. Though they had only exchanged a few words, the king and queen were kind. Their eyes were full of hope. And Jasyn... She was drawn to him. He looked ruffled and unkempt with no shoes on his feet, yet he still sat regal on his throne.

"You did well for a window washer."

Iskra stiffened at Bron's voice. He and Esi had spent yesterday teaching her everything they could before today's appearance, including how to mimic Esi's friendly voice, though Iskra didn't think she succeeded. It wasn't enough time to truly learn how to exude a noble-born lady, which was why walking in those heels had been treacherous, but it provided her with enough to get through her entrance. Now, Bron was going to use whatever private moment they had to continue those lessons. Esi was already off gallivanting with her secret lover for the day, but she promised to return tonight.

"Luckily, it was short," Iskra replied.

Bron now stood next to two glass doors to a balcony. "I asked for a room on the first floor to allow you and Esi to switch easily, but they didn't seem to take my request into consideration." One of the maids had informed them this was the best room in the castle, outside of those already occupied by the royal family—though once the marriage was consummated, Esi would be moved in Jasyn's room.

Iskra joined Bron but opened the doors and headed outside. The balcony was covered in vines, and it overlooked a garden. Or gardens, she should say. The whole castle grounds were covered in bushes, flowers, and trees. She breathed in deeply, the smells stronger because of her shifting abilities, her senses overwhelmed by the scent. Not in a bad way, but it reminded her of how much existed outside the walls of Kryth's shop and how little she had experienced.

"I don't mind the height," Iskra said.

"You say that now, but when it comes time for you and Esi to climb up and down, it's going to create a challenge."

"We can use the curtains to create a rope."

"I don't think the royals would appreciate us using their stuff like that."

"You don't seem to like Esi's plan."

Bron crossed his arms, showing off his muscles. He only wore a vest, the chest plate steel. "I'm not able to keep my eyes on Esi. If she gets hurt, it will be my fault. Plus, I don't trust that shop owner of yours." Bron shivered. "Apothecaries like to promise one thing but deliver on another. I don't trust him—and, by extension, you."

Iskra took him in. Bron wasn't wrong for distrusting Kryth. Iskra didn't trust him either, and in every spare moment, she wondered why exactly Kryth had allowed her to participate in this plan.

Then, Iskra wondered about Bron's relationship with Esi and how fiercely he protected her. It couldn't just be loyalty and fear making him clutch his duties tightly. Was it love, obsession, or something entirely self-motivated? Iskra didn't have enough time to figure it out quite yet.

"Good thing Esi will be back for dinner." Even though the sun set late in the Sun Court, Esi promised to return earlier to at least acquaint herself with the man she was destined to marry.

He ignored Iskra. "I'm going to my room. It's across the hall. If she doesn't show up or if you need anything, knock three times. I'll know it's you."

Bron left her, and all Iskra could do was anchor her head back and allow the sun to shine on her skin. She savored its warmth, because in a few short weeks, when Jasyn and Esi married, Iskra would just be ash in the wind.

Three

Iskra's right buttock was sore from switching with Esi last night. Esi had struggled to climb up the roped sheets Iskra had thrown down to her, and it had required Bron and Iskra to heave her up as slyly as possible, which was a difficult feat. Once Esi had made it to the other side of the balcony, she swore under her breath.

"There has to be an easier way," Esi had mumbled as she wiped at the leaves clinging to her dress.

"I should go," Iskra had responded, quickly taking the sheet, tying it to the balcony, and sliding down, only to land ungracefully on her backside. But sunset had been on the brink of night, and Iskra had needed to rush.

When she returned to the shop, Kryth had been waiting by the door, his arms crossed and a scowl on his face. Shortly after they got inside, darkness swept over the court, and Iskra's body shifted, her fingertips and toes tingling. Back into the small cage she went.

Today, at new light, Iskra tip-toed back to the castle. Undoubtedly, Esi had left for the day, so Iskra needed to make it there before anyone noticed.

Before she'd left the shop—wearing a green lace dress, which would have suited her auburn hair better—Iskra had looked at herself in the mirror. Even if only her hair color and texture had been the features to change, she barely recognized herself.

She was weaving through the bramble in another pair of uncomfortable heels when she heard grunts and heaves. Curious, Iskra made her way toward the noise, still in awe of the castle grounds. Everything felt so intentional, yet she was inclined to believe the roots grew of their own volition, whatever way Goddess Slone desired. The castle workers just ensured everything was well-kept.

On the other side of an iron-wrought gate, Prince Jasyn stood in the center of a courtyard. There was no one else in sight, but she doubted he wasn't being watched by his guard from some veiled angle.

Iskra hunched so she could hide as she watched.

He slashed a sword against no opponent, his movements quick and light. They flowed like the weapon was an extension of those toned, golden brown arms. She would have considered it beautiful had she not thought about *why* he was training. She was ready to move along to her room when the unexpected happened.

Jasyn spun and kicked, and when he made it back around, he projected his free hand out. A sliver of light bloomed from his palm—a graceful, quiet wave of light.

Iskra gasped and stumbled in her heeled shoes, the sound of swaying leaves unforgiving. Jasyn whipped his attention in her direction, and she knew she was caught.

"Lady Esi?" His voice was hesitant, unsure, perhaps even shy.

Iskra pushed back the strand of hair that had fallen in her face and finally got the courage to move from her hiding place. She knew Bron would be livid when he heard about this.

Iskra cleared her throat as she entered the courtyard, the hinges of the gate squeaking behind her.

"Prince Jasyn," she curtsied.

Jasyn put the sword back in its sheath at his hip. "What are you doing out so early?"

"I could ask you the same."

"This is my home," he countered, and she decided not to bring up how this was Esi's home now too.

She barely knew this man, but he didn't seem to be someone who used many words. In the quiet moment, she took him in. He was dressed in a tunic and flowy pants, clothes not particularly made for fighting and slaying.

"That's a neat trick." Iskra pointed to his hand.

He looked down at his palm, like he had no clue what she was talking about.

"The light. Though I don't believe that will be helpful when it comes time to slay the dragon."

Jasyn kept quiet, so Iskra kept talking.

"I never realized such magic existed in this court. I thought it was only flames."

Still, nothing from him. Was he ashamed? He wasn't even looking at her.

"This training might also be more helpful if you had an opponent," she continued, only saying things to disturb the silence. She was tired of the quiet. She'd spent too many years in her head. Now that she had a reprieve, she wanted to fill the world with her words. A whiplash of memories hit her: of being in the fields as a young girl, her mouth blabbering and her mother shushing her for some peace. She blinked, preferring to avoid thinking too much about the past, before Kryth stole her away from her home, the brand a magicked mark on her skin cursing her to shift each night and a way to keep track of her movements.

"I like training alone," Jasyn said.

He speaks, she thought. Still not a lot of words, but enough to keep the conversation flowing. Esi had told her that on top of pretending to be Lady Esi, Iskra should also try to woo the prince. This marriage was advantageous for both her and the royal family, so even though Esi had wanted a small sliver of freedom before marriage, she was committed to making this work when the time came.

"You're very good with that sword," Iskra praised in hopes of him responding. Esi had mentioned men thrived on compliments.

"Is—" He swallowed. "Is there something I can help you with?"

He *was* nervous. He had seemed confident yesterday, but perhaps that was just a show for his parents. Or maybe it was something deeper.

"To answer your earlier question, I'm out this early because of the freedom."

"Freedom?"

Iskra nodded. "I'm sure you must know what it's like to be duty-bound, how it can feel like a cage. I've been in my own cage my whole life. It's freeing to be outside it."

That was a light way of describing her current situation.

"I've been lucky enough to have a key to my cage. My siblings were the ones stuck inside theirs," Jasyn explained.

She dipped her head. "I'm sorry for your loss."

He shrugged. "It's not your fault."

And yet, Iskra felt like it was.

He sighed looking down at his hand. "My power is unique, and it would be wise you keep it to yourself."

"Was that a threat?"

Jasyn snorted, and his nose crinkled. She wondered how he would look if he fully and freely laughed. It must be a contagious sight, because although he seemed to shrink into himself, there was still something composed and regal about his presence. He captured her attention and held it.

"I don't think it would go well for me if I threatened my future wife. It was only a suggestion."

"It's beautiful. I don't know why you would want to hide it."

A warm gust of wind blew, and Iskra's skirt billowed while her hair attacked her face. She went to brush it back from her lips, but Jasyn was there, pushing it away before she could. Usually, the sudden contact would cause her to flinch, but something about Jasyn only calmed her. She blinked her amber eyes at him, and her heart stuttered at his solemnity.

"My power is not what it has once been." His voice was raw, pained. She could tell he was uncomfortable. Yet, she didn't want this conversation to end. There was something so normal about talking to him, even if he was a prince.

"Do you do everything alone?" she asked, trying to change the direction of the conversation.

"Most things. Sometimes with Mych, but he's usually busy being a guard."

Iskra snorted. A colorful butterfly flitted past her and landed directly on Jasyn's shoulder.

He must have noticed her longing expression, because he asked, "Do you ever get out?"

"Not often." She smiled sadly. She didn't know if she should be this vocal about the isolation she had personally experienced. After all, Lady Esi no doubt lived a life filled with parties and other social responsibilities.

"We can change that. *I* can change that."

Iskra raised her brows. "What do you get out of it?"

"Getting to know my future wife like I promised I would yesterday."

"Right..."

She liked the sound of it, but in practice, she feared what it would do to her when it came time to leave this all behind. This luxurious life would spoil her, but it was an opportunity to experience something new before it all ended, and she would claim it.

"Let's do it," she said more confidently, right as the butterfly flew away. "Maybe we'll even find you some new friends. A king must have allies in his court."

"I'll have you and your family's side," he reminded her.

"Of course, but this court is larger than me and you. I'm ready to see it and for you to embrace it."

He nodded, as if he could find no other argument against her statement. "To learning about each other as we learn about the court we will rule together, then."

He extended his hand, and this time, Iskra didn't hesitate as she took it. He smiled at her, and Iskra's breath hitched at the sight. Right then, she promised herself not to get attached to the man in front of her. It would only break her when she had to let this all go.

Dirt was caught beneath Jasyn's nails. The afternoon sun blazed heat on his back, but it never bothered him. Perhaps the sun recognized the innate light within Jasyn, how they were one and the same, despite how death and grief had stolen the core of his full potential.

Jasyn heard the rumble of wheels before he saw his father.

"Another day with your plants?" his father asked, and although he meant it in a teasing manner, it grated on Jasyn's nerves. "What have they told you today?"

It was an ongoing joke, one started by Jaymes, his oldest sibling. When Jasyn was a child, he would talk animatedly to the plants. Every night at dinner, Jaymes would ask what the plants told him.

"Is there something I can do for you?" This was the second time in one day someone had disturbed him. His days had been a lot quieter with his siblings now dead, and he had grown accustomed to that silence. He had liked when Lady Esi had appeared, though. Their conversation had been vulnerable, and he saw a potential of a future with her, which was both relieving and terrifying.

His father pushed the wheelchair over so he had a view of what Jasyn had been working on. The small pile of weeds didn't scream interesting.

"I heard you had a visitor during training."

Jasyn swallowed; he should have known word would have spread about his encounter with Lady Esi. "Yes."

"Does she know about your light?"

"Yes."

His father sighed deeply. His parents had kept his power a secret since he was a babe. He was only a few months old when he shined so brightly, his mother almost dropped him. They weren't ashamed of Jasyn's power, but they feared the court wouldn't take him seriously since he didn't have fire. The light that poured from his hands was like sunlight, blinding and bright—though more dim now. It was different from the powers of the lightning court, the electricity that buzzed with energy.

"She's to be my wife. I think she has a right to know," Jasyn explained.

"I still would have preferred waiting until the marriage was sealed."

"She doesn't seem turned off by it."

"No?"

"She seemed intrigued," Jasyn continued. He wanted to tell his father they already had a deal to spend more time together. Jaymes and Dahlia would be proud of him; as much as they joked about how the plants were Jasyn's only friends, they were genuinely concerned he would never be able to lead because he didn't have the charm. He hoped spending time with Esi would help him gain confidence.

"You still have a lot of training ahead of you," his father said seriously. "Without fire, you'll be relying on your sword more to slay that beast and win us the Undertaking."

Jasyn tried not to roll his eyes. "I'm aware."

"As evidenced by where I sit, that's not an easy feat, but it's not impossible."

When his father watched Jaymes die during the Undertaking—the one his father had hoped would have crowned his eldest son as king—his father had stepped up and started training more. He wanted to compete in the Undertaking using only his sword to see if Jasyn had a chance of winning in case Dahlia didn't survive. His father had won the Undertaking after doing exactly that. Two years after Jaymes' death, Dahlia entered the Undertaking along with their father, and she died while King Aleks prevailed. He had been so badly injured, his legs no longer moved; this family's legacy only continued because other competitors decided to offer a helping hand to his father out of loyalty to the throne. Now, it was up to Jasyn. Unlike his siblings, his father wouldn't be competing alongside him as back up.

"I'm ready to slay the dragon and win this family the crown again."

His father patted his arm. "Good. I expect nothing less."

Four

Iskra coughed as she entered the tobacco-scented shop. Kryth dangled a mouse in front of one of the cages, and Iskra saw one of the small dragons eyeing it, growling with starvation. She gulped, knowing exactly how it felt.

"I'm back," she announced, but Iskra had no doubt Kryth felt her presence as soon as she had turned the corner to this street—not only because of the brand on her skin, but because of his Sight. Kryth could only see what the Gods wanted him to, but for whatever reason, his gift also made him extra sensitive to his surroundings. Perhaps those enhanced senses were what allowed him to find a hoard of dragons to capture.

Kryth peered outside the window to where the sun was on the edge of the horizon. The sky was almost completely blue for the night.

"Just in time," he said simply as he approached the empty cage and opened the door for her. It was a humiliating sight. "We can't have a dragon on the loose."

Iskra wanted to protest, even if she knew it would be in vain. She had always wondered why Kryth didn't let the dragons live in their full sizes in some secluded cave as they awaited their doomed fates. It was already cruel enough that the shifters were stuck in their dragon forms. Locking them up like that took it to another extreme.

"How's our future king?" Kryth asked as he puffed on his pipe. He didn't seem excited by the prospect of Jasyn winning. Iskra wondered then where Kryth's loyalties lied. Was it with the Gods, or did he want to see someone succeed each year and take the crown?

"He's still mourning." Iskra felt like that was a safe enough statement to make. Both of his siblings had died within the past three years, and his father was now disabled because of the Undertaking. She didn't dare utter a word about the light that had flooded from his hands. Even if Jasyn didn't tell her to keep it to herself, the last person she would pass the information to would be Kryth. She realized then, though, that Esi needed to be informed so she wasn't surprised by it later.

"He'll need to toughen up if he expects to kill you." Kryth's sharp words pierced something within her.

She knew Kryth said the words as a reminder. *This was temporary.* In a few weeks, she would be in that Undertaking cave, protecting the ruby Heart while Jasyn and other competitors fought to kill her to claim the throne.

Decades ago, it was required that the king or queen participated in the Undertaking. One year, the king at the time refused and begged the minister to speak to the Gods about opening up the pool of competition. He would give up his title so he didn't have to risk his life anymore. The Gods obliged him—with a catch. Since then, anyone over the age of twenty could enter, but whomever won the Heart was crowned ruler. King Aleks had been competing and winning for almost two decades.

Each year, a new dragon was picked to protect the Heart. This year, Iskra had the honor to do it. It was why she was allowed this sliver of freedom before her slaughter.

"He'll do it." Iskra didn't know if she believed the words. Jasyn seemed nervous, soft. That wouldn't bode well when a dragon was coming at him, especially if he didn't have a lick of flame in his veins.

"I hope you're right." Kryth gestured for her to get in the cage. "It would be a shame if this court burned to the ground."

Iskra reached, and as the last bit of light disappeared for the night, she morphed into something *other*. Her body flew inside the small cage, and Kryth locked her inside for the night.

Cherry blossoms guided him to his least favorite place. Jasyn passed by the headstones of all the competitors who had died during the Undertaking. They were honored with a burial on the castle grounds for their bravery. Many of those deep within the ground were the reason his father still ruled today. Yet, he barely spared them a glance. He had one destination in mind.

The sun had set for the night, engulfing the gazebo mausoleum in darkness. Esi had gone to bed early. His parents decided to go on a short trip to the border with the Lightning Court.

Although Jasyn thrived in the sunlight, the quiet of night always provided him a sense of peace. Even as a child, he would sneak out to explore the castle grounds, and sometimes, he even went as far as going into town. It was on one of those occasions when he was alone, weaving through the pebbly streets, when he manifested his powers in front of people outside his family.

He had stumbled upon a large crowd and hid behind a carriage as he watched a group play some game with a ball until it landed close to another, smaller ball. Jasyn had been intrigued, so he hadn't been paying attention. Someone grabbed him from behind, but before Jasyn even caught a glimpse of the person, he had beamed with light. The person had let go of him as they yelled about their eyes, and Jasyn ran home without looking back. Thankfully, no one seemed to tattle about what they saw.

Perhaps he was never scared of the dark because of the light inside him. If he was alone, he had his power to depend on, even in its weaker state. Every day, he attempted to beam like he once could and failed, just like he would fail as king if he won the Undertaking. What court would want a man who preferred plants over humans as their ruler? He ignored those thoughts, like he had for the past year after Dahlia's death, when he realized he was the last option for this family to continue their legacy.

Jasyn didn't need that light now anyway. He opened the door to the enclosed gazebo and shut it behind him. Smoky incense hit his nostrils in a wave. Heading deeper inside, he didn't look at the bronze plaques on the floor. He had memorized the names and placements of the former Sun Court rulers, so he headed directly to the two who had meant the most to him.

Jaymes and Dahlia.

Technically, since Jaymes and Dahlia had never actually ruled, they weren't meant to be honored with their names in the mausoleum, but they had been part of the royal family, so it only made sense they were remembered here. Their bodies were now burned to ash and lost to the wind, but they would forever be stamped in memory.

Would Jasyn's name join theirs in a few weeks? Or would he live long enough to see his parents' names? He didn't know what option sounded better, but he did know he wanted to make his parents, siblings, and the court proud. All it required was slaying a dragon and swiping the Heart it protected.

Jasyn placed a bouquet of flowers on each of the plaques.

"Our legacy will continue," Jasyn promised his brother and sister. "Even in death, I feel your presence, and I will not let this family down."

Now, with only a few weeks left, he needed to prove he deserved to be king.

Five

With his parents gone, Jasyn considered cancelling on Esi. He had to protect the castle, he would tell her. He couldn't leave the premises empty. When Mych heard his poor excuses, he told the entire guard unit to be on extra alert as Prince Jasyn left the grounds for a few hours.

Jasyn wanted to shake his friend, but as soon as Esi stepped into the courtyard, that anger dissolved.

She looked like a queen. The simple linen dress was tight on her chest but flared outwards, reaching below her knees. The navy color accentuated the tan of her skin, and in the sun, he noticed the freckles along her cheeks. She swiped back her wavy tresses half up while the rest flowed across her back. The dark color was like an inky sea, enticing him to touch it.

Jasyn's heart stalled at the sight. He clearly was staring, because he saw the faint blush beginning to form beneath her freckles.

"What?" she asked, patting her face as if something was on it.

He shook himself out of it. "Nothing." His morning voice was scratchy. "You look beautiful."

If he planned on winning the court over, he might as well practice his charm—or lack thereof—on Esi. So far, he noticed he needed to expand his compliment vocabulary. She was beyond beautiful. She was like stepping into a meadow of sundrops in the morning, just as the sun peeked over the horizon and the flowers bloomed.

Wiping at her skirt, she looked down at herself. "Thank you. The material is perfect for this warm day."

"Every day is warm here." He cringed. He should have kept that to himself.

But she laughed, and the sound hit something deep within him. "I suppose you're right."

He extended his arm, offering it to her. "Ready?"

She turned to look behind her, where Bron and Mych both stood, prepared to follow them into town. Bron nodded, and she breathed deeply before linking her arm with Jaysn's.

As they walked, Esi informed him there was no plan. When he looked at her with concern, she squeezed his arm.

"Your goal should be to be spontaneous with your people. They should not feel like a duty you must fulfill, but rather like they are an extension of you. They support this court, allowing it to thrive. Now, it's up to you to show your thanks and care."

Jasyn cocked his head as they passed by shops, the owners flipping their signs over to 'open.' He rarely ventured out to town this early, preferring to spend his morning tending to the gardens.

He allowed Esi's words to burrow into his mind. She had a point. The royal family didn't matter if the people were not there to support this court. It was important to build a strong bond with them, especially because there had been court members who entered the Undertaking with the goal of helping his father win. They loved King Aleks and Queen Kait and wanted their rulership to continue. That was loyalty his parents had created through their years as monarchs, something Jasyn wanted to emulate if he became king.

They neared the town square where there was a large fountain. The sun reflected a rainbow against the water, and children ran in and out of the cascade. Then, there were adults roaming the streets, bouncing from one shop to another, carrying baskets of dirty clothes to the nearby lake to clean. Jasyn tried not thinking about the sun that beat down, or the loud noises, or the fact that people were looking at him as he walked with Esi.

He knew Esi was waving. She even let go of him to crouch down to a child's height, accepting a dandelion from a small boy, who gave her a toothy smile. He smiled back at the child, but it must have not come off kindly, because the boy began to cry. He ran off, and Jasyn swallowed, trying not to be hurt by it.

"It's because you're so tall," Esi joked from beside him as she walked up to a fruit stand.

Jasyn chuckled, but it was a forced sound. He let Esi speak with the fruit seller, as words were failing him right now. Everything around him was moving too quickly and too slowly at the same time. A blur and a standstill. He tried moving forward, but his legs felt glued to the ground. When he tried taking a deep breath, it was like his chest was locked up, unable to take any air.

"Are you okay?"

He knew those were words directed at him. He recognized the female voice. He liked who it belonged to, but his body refused to respond. Warmth touched his arm gently, and he gazed down at the tan hand. The contrast of Esi's flesh against his golden brown skin reminded him of why he was here.

"I'm fine," he finally managed to say, or at least he thought he did. His mouth felt disconnected from his body.

"Let's go in there." She gestured her head toward a shop, but he didn't care where they went as long as it was away from the crowd.

He heard two sets of footsteps following them, but right before they entered the building, Esi turned.

"Maybe it's best if it's just us." She smiled at Bron and Mych.

Mych opened his mouth, ready to stop them, but Jasyn was able to jerk his head to indicate his guard didn't need to follow. Jasyn knew Mych would not be happy leaving Jasyn alone. Esi didn't give them another moment to protest before she took Jasyn's hand and led him inside.

Iskra was blasted with heat as she stepped inside the unidentified shop. The smell of wax and musk overwhelmed her senses as she slowly put together where they were.

"Glass," Jasyn said. It was only one word, but Iskra could sense calmness in his voice. His panic was beginning to burn out, and she took a shuddering breath of relief. What happened out there was a surprise. She never would expect a future king to struggle so deeply with being surrounded by his people. When she asked Esi for suggestions for today, she was the one who mentioned letting him engage with his people in a natural way. It was exactly why she needed to get him out of sight. If the arranged marriage was meant to instill confidence in the royal family, then Iskra needed to make sure to keep that image alive.

As they stood at the entrance to the glass blowing facility, Iskra couldn't help but pity the man beside her.

"Slone will not let me escape glass," Iskra muttered to herself, wanting to avoid speaking about what just transpired. She had a feeling Jasyn wouldn't want to speak on it either.

"Prince Jasyn," a man's voice said as he approached them with thick gloves on, his eyes wide with disbelief. The shock must have quickly worn off as he remembered himself. The glassblower bowed deeply and focused his attention on her. "You must be the queen-to-be, Lady Esi."

Iskra opened her mouth to correct him, but then she remembered the role she was playing. It was still hard pretending to be someone else, to hide her identity when she was already hiding an even bigger part of herself.

"That is me," she said, and the words must have not sounded convincing, because the man raised one of his brows. "Prince Jasyn and I were walking through town and stumbled upon the glasswork in your window."

Iskra pointed behind her to the display she had actually missed when she guided Jasyn inside, and the gesture didn't feel ladylike.

Jasyn seemed to have settled down, because he stepped in. "I have always been curious about how one could use their flame powers to craft such intricate work. I grew up being taught my flame should be forged to fight and kill a dragon. Here, you have created art."

Although she wasn't surprised his light powers were a secret, it still hurt something within her to hear Jasyn lie about himself.

"Oh, how kind," the glassblower said. "Of course I can demonstrate. I have wine glasses Princess Syrena from the Rain Court commissioned for her new home with some pirate."

"I didn't realize the Rain Court had royalty." The words were out before she could stop them.

Both the glassblower and Jasyn turned to her.

"Only the seafolk have royalty," Jasyn explained. "Though it's practically meaningless when so many mermaids are bestowed a title. Only our court and the Snow Court have formal royalty, since the other courts have progressed beyond such a government. Even then, our court is less formal." Iskra listened, taking in each word. She appreciated how willing he was to answer questions she hadn't even asked yet. It was the most she heard him speak in the few days she'd known him.

"Let's start," the glassblower interjected as he headed to a large furnace. "This furnace is constantly lit and maintained."

He went through each step, described what he was doing, and even allowed them to help. They simply turned the pipe as the glassblower used his power to heat the glass and bend it into a specific shape. This specific glass had a marbled effect with various tones of green.

Throughout it all, Iskra kept her eyes on Jasyn. He was much more at ease when he worked with his hands. Perhaps that was why she caught him tending to the garden so often. There must be a sense of safety with motion for him.

After finishing the wine glass, they moved on to making a vase. The glassblower gestured for her to blow through the pipe, but she tried refusing. He wouldn't have it, and she slowly placed her mouth on the mouthpiece, gently blowing. She held back the fire within her, unsure if she could even call it in this form yet still determined to make sure it stayed put.

When Jasyn did it, she watched as he placed his mouth where hers just was, and she tried to ignore the bubbly feeling in her stomach. The glassblower gasped, and Jasyn laughed as the hollow ball they had formed drooped. She snorted, and Jasyn's smile turned to her. She dipped her head, facing away, unable to take the joy lighting his face. If she kept getting lost in him, she feared she would never be able to find her way out again.

The glassblower finished some final steps. Iskra didn't have the mind to pay too close attention, but the glassblower revealed their work. Clearly, he had fixed Jasyn's mishap but kept the charm, because it had the curve Jasyn had made. The shades of red were stunning in the sunlight once they finally left the shop.

"It's perfect," she said, the creation in her arms.

Jasyn stopped, and she was scared he would panic again, but he only reached out and pulled back the hair from in front of her face. Her eyes tracked his hands—she should really pull away. It was dangerous how that small act twisted her insides. "Thank you for giving me the space to breathe."

Iskra blinked, taking in his vulnerability. She opened her mouth to say more, but his guard—who had been dutifully waiting while they were in the shop—stepped in.

"I think it's time to return to the castle," Mych said.

Jasyn stepped back, and she looked down at the vase in her hands. She didn't know why she was feeling shy. Everyone knew Jasyn and Esi were to be married. It made sense that they were close.

She then looked at Bron, and he wore a stone-cold face. He was not impressed, or perhaps watching her be with Jasyn reminded him that his friend—the real Lady Esi—would be in her spot in a few weeks.

If Jasyn could survive the Undertaking, at least.

Six

As the carriage rattled back to the castle, Iskra twiddled her fingers. Her fingernails were painted crimson, her hands adorned with gold jewelry. It was how Lady Esi dressed every day. It was still foreign to Iskra to see such finery on herself, but she liked how it made her feel—like she was more than just a body built for slaughter.

The sun began to dip beneath the horizon, and if she didn't get out soon, everyone would be in for a surprise.

Bron noticed her nerves, because he asked, "Can we make this move faster?"

Mych gave him a curious glare. "Are you so bothered by our company?"

Bron opened his mouth, likely to make some inappropriate retort.

"I get nauseous easily," Iskra jumped in before the two guards began to brawl.

"Next time, we'll make sure to bring some mint leaves for you to chew on. I have a whole garden dedicated to herbs."

Iskra smiled at Jasyn. He sat across from her, and she was careful not to tap her knees against his, but with the roughness of the road, it was a tricky feat.

He smiled back at her, and his skin practically glowed. She didn't know if it was his power or just the sun seeping through the window. Whichever it was, it didn't make it easier for her to ignore his allure.

"We're almost there," Jasyn assured her, and she could practically cry at his kindness in the few days she had known him. Even if he didn't have the qualities one would expect for a ruler, she had no doubts the people would love him. They just needed a chance to get to know him for *him*.

Jasyn was right; the rest of the journey was quick. He helped her out of the carriage, and when their hands connected, she had to hide the sharp inhale of breath.

"I'll bring you some flowers and water for the vase tonight," Jasyn said nervously.

Iskra blinked but then remembered what she held. "Tonight?"

He nodded, biting his bottom lip. He was unsure, and she wasn't making it easier on him.

Iskra watched as the sun sank, close to leaving for the night. Her heart raced. She needed to leave soon.

"Prince Jasyn, I had the most wonderful day, and it has left me tired. I feel like I need to rest. Does tomorrow work?"

He hesitated, as if hurt by the way she pushed back. Guilt clawed at her, but she had no choice. It was a reminder that no matter how much she pretended she was free, Kryth still had power over her.

"Of course, Lady Esi. You deserve to rest."

She hated *that* name coming from his lips. She wanted it to be *hers*, and she didn't care if those thoughts were selfish, even if it was the most dangerous thing of all.

"Until then." She curtsied, though the movement was awkward. She really needed to practice

Bron practically yanked her away. Once there was enough distance between them and the prince and his guard, under his breath, Bron scolded her. "You're playing with fire."

Iskra could have bent back her head and laughed at the irony. He had no idea how well aware Iskra was of the situation.

Iskra shoved away a branch, and as she passed it, it swung back, right into Bron's face. He grabbed her arm and forced her to face him. His dark eyes looked ready to pop out of his sockets.

"This game was started by the person you're meant to protect," she seethed as she poked his chest hard. She was doing Esi a favor. Whether Bron liked it was not Iskra's problem. He could puff his chest out and actually talk with Esi if he was that concerned.

As if the words had beckoned her, the real Esi stumbled from the bushes.

"Oh, you're here," Esi said, her voice light and content. Iskra and Bron backed away from each other. "Is something wrong?"

"Nothing," Iskra said.

"She's falling for him," Bron announced.

Iskra opened her mouth and shut it, her teeth clanging. She huffed in frustration.

"Here." Iskra gave Esi the vase. "We made it this afternoon at a shop together. He was overwhelmed by crowds, so we rushed away. Also, his power—" Iskra stopped herself. For some reason, she didn't want to reveal it to either of them, especially Bron. It felt like betraying Jasyn. But Esi should know...

"What about it?" Esi pushed as she turned the vase in her hands, investigating the colors and shape.

"He's powerful," Iskra managed to say. "I must go."

Before she could reconsider, she left the two of them.

Jasyn watched Esi and her guard disappear into the trees, and he was left standing there. Alone.

"You did good today," Mych said.

"Don't mock me," the words came out sharp, and he sighed at himself. "Apologies. That was uncalled for."

Mych chuckled. "I'm serious. The way she was looking at you tells me she's smitten."

"I panicked in front of the people, *my* people. I doubt she is looking fondly at me. She's likely laughing at me now, wondering how I'm meant to be king."

"Stop pitying yourself," his guard said. "You were not trained for this role like Jaymes and Dahlia. You're learning."

Jasyn should have been learning long ago with his siblings. No one had expected him to need to, though, and it left him in a vulnerable position. He wasn't guaranteed the throne, but he wanted it. He wanted to win the Undertaking, to have his father give him the crown. But what if the people didn't want him? What if Esi didn't want to marry him? He was beginning to feel something towards the lady. She was different. They had only known each other a few days, but she seemed to understand him in a way no one else did.

"I see your mind spinning. Perhaps, like Lady Esi, it's time for bed," Mych reasoned.

"I'm going to visit her," Jasyn said.

"I don't think that's a good idea."

He didn't listen to his friend. He went to the garden to pluck an arrangement of flowers and headed to her room. He knocked twice and waited. In those few seconds, doubt creeped in, but he didn't want to lose his momentum.

The door opened, and there she was. She was in a different dress from earlier, and he eyed it with narrow eyes.

"Good evening, my prince." She curtsied, the movement fluid and easy. Had she been practicing since they parted?

"Good evening. I know you mentioned you were headed to bed, but I wanted to give you these."

He passed over the flowers. She didn't seem excited about them. Then, he realized there were a few in the bouquet that hadn't bloomed.

"I wanted to give you them tonight because those," he pointed to the bulbs, "will sprout in the morning. They'll close again at night when the sun is gone."

Esi blinked, like her mind was elsewhere, barely taking in his words, but she quickly adjusted herself back to the present. "They're lovely. I'll make sure to put them in the vase."

They stood quietly, both staring at each other, and Jasyn's stomach dropped. There was something off. He didn't feel the tug like he usually did around Esi. He rubbed at his chest, as if that would fix it.

"I also wanted to say I appreciate that you have kept what you have learned about my power private."

Esi's mouth opened and shut, and he could read the confusion. Esi had rambled about his powers when she witnessed them in the garden that one morning, so he was concerned by her lack of memory of the encounter.

"This." He opened his palm, and a faint light glowed from it.

Her eyes widened, like she was seeing it for the first time. He closed his palm again. Instead of the usual delightful pull, there was an eerie nagging starting to form. Something was wrong.

"I'll let you rest now, Lady Esi. Apologies for the interruption."

She smiled, and it wasn't the same. The pattern of her freckles seemed to have shifted. What was wrong? "No apologies required. Good night, Prince Jasyn."

He turned to go, but right as he did, he heard the click of Bron's door. Had he been listening? Maybe he was just overprotective.

Jasyn shook it off. It was likely just the exhaustion finally catching up to him. He needed sleep.

Seven

Iskra blew the feather fan in the bright—very early—sun. It beamed down on her like a spotlight, and even in the thin, linen dress, her body was coated in sweat.

She and Bron were seated next to each other within what the royal family deemed 'The Weather Gods garden,' which described the location perfectly. Large wooden gates surrounded them, with wisteria and vines enclosing the crowd. At each corner was a statue of one of the Weather Gods, and in the center was a statue of Goddess Slone. All the chairs circled the sun goddess.

Jasyn sat with his parents in the front while a few other guests also joined them, though Iskra did not have a clue who they were.

Within the beauty and peace of the garden, Iskra had to focus on a chilling stain: Kryth. He had transformed himself to the role of minister. His silver hair shone in the sun, his skin youthful. She rarely saw him in this form, and it always surprised her how those subtle shifts made him appear so much more otherworldly than his shop owner form.

Bron clearly didn't like the sight of the minister either. He squirmed in his seat, his eyes like two blades ready to strike.

"What's wrong with you?" Iskra hissed, slapping the fan on Bron's thigh when he grumbled deep in his throat.

Bron whipped his head in her direction, those violent eyes now on her. "Nothing," he snapped. "Keep to yourself."

"The minister is not going to do anything to you."

Bron clenched his jaw. "Who's to say he hasn't already?"

Iskra's mouth opened, but before she could question him further, Kryth began to preach.

Iskra zoned out, uninterested in what he had to say about the gods and their goodness. If the gods were truly benevolent, Iskra wouldn't need to die for them and this court.

Instead, Iskra eyed Jasyn. His posture was straight and his eyes focused, but she could see the nerves coursing through him even from here. He fiddled with his hands, and once she squinted, Iskra saw he was holding something. She couldn't see clearly, but it was a round object.

She wished then that she could comfort him, to remind him she was here, that he wasn't alone. Yet...the small distance between them felt like a whole ocean. So, she sat politely, acting like a noble lady instead of the brewing beast that desired to escape the clutches of duty.

Sometimes, Jasyn wished his family wasn't royalty—that his father never chose to enter the Undertaking and leave victorious for decades. His parents could have chosen a cottage in the outskirts of the court, where it was quiet. He and his siblings would be able to freely roam without potentially life-ending responsibilities weighing on them. Jaymes and Dahlia would still be here, and Jasyn wouldn't need to listen to the minister of the Sun Court drone on about the Weather Gods.

Then, it would be like cold water had been poured on him as he remembered the honor and privilege of being able to sit in this position, how he actually enjoyed the work involved in running a court.

Once the minister made his closing remarks and the crowd began to disperse, Jasyn practically jumped from his seat and stretched. Not being able to move for an hour had left him antsy.

"You never grew out of those childhood traits, did you?" his father asked as he turned to face his son.

Jasyn shrugged, his eyes immediately landing on Esi. Unlike last night, the pull was back, and he sighed in relief.

"Being king means you'll need to become accustomed to sitting for a long time. And if your fate is like mine, you'll be seated forever."

Those words pulled Jasyn's attention away from Esi, who was speaking to her guard. Jasyn cleared his throat, unsure of the words to respond. While grieving Dahlia, his father also had to grieve the life he'd once lived. Jasyn couldn't imagine the pain of it all.

"Don't pity me, son," his father said sternly. "Amidst the grief for my two children and my worry for you, I am still living a full life, even in this chair. It has allowed me to slow down in ways I needed."

His mother must have finished her conversation with Kryth, because she was at Jasyn's side, wrapping her arms around his shoulder and pressing a kiss to his temple.

"I think your father deserves time to rest after years of leading," she said.

Jasyn took in his parents. They had given so much of their lives for this court, and now, it was Jasyn's turn.

"Will you join us for lunch?" His mother's question was hopeful.

Jasyn nodded but let his eyes wander to Esi. The minister was now with her and Bron. Bron looked ready to tackle the minister any second.

"I'll be there soon," Jasyn told his parents, and they both gave him a secretive smile when they noticed the direction of his eyes.

"Be good," his mother jokingly warned, and Jasyn batted away both his parents before they teased him anymore.

Approaching Esi, Jasyn heard the tail end of the minister's words.

"The Gods have chosen such a beautiful bride for our next king."

Esi didn't seem to enjoy the compliment, because she looked to be biting her tongue as he reached the group. Mych stood guard at the entrance to the garden, but his eyes were on Bron, as if he, too, noticed his discomfort.

"The Gods chose a vile minister," Bron snapped, as if he couldn't hold in the words anymore, as if he was a volcano ready to burst.

Kryth smiled, and it wasn't warm. A chill went down Jasyn's spine. He didn't have anything against the minister, but something about the man seemed sinister.

The minister cocked his head. "You seem familiar."

Jasyn looked back at Mych, who was already stalking over, as if he sensed the distress beginning to bubble.

"You're a fraud with only words as your shield." Bron had his arm on the hilt of his sword, ready to unleash it from its sheath. "Lucky for me, I have steel."

"Siena could not be saved."

Bron's face immediately blanched. "Don't you dare utter my mother's name."

Jasyn was bouncing his head between the two of them, taking in the conversation. Mych was at Bron's side now. "I'll escort you off the premises, sir." The words, directed at Kryth, were cordial and professional, but there was an underlying sternness. Jasyn had never heard Mych use such a tone.

The minister eyed the four of them, but he lingered on Bron and then stared at Esi. Jasyn felt the urge to pull her away from the man.

"Life is such a fickle thing. It's a shame it's cut so short for many."

Jasyn could feel Esi tense next to him.

Then, Kryth left. Jasyn watched Mych and the minister go, and Bron stormed off shortly after, leaving just Esi and him alone together.

Esi had her arms around herself, as if she was spooked. Jasyn wanted to reach out and bring her close, but he kept his distance. "I apologize for Krytn."

Esi snapped out of whatever daze she was in as she faced him. She curtsied, and he hated the sight of it.

"No need for formalities, Esi." He assumed they had moved past that after yesterday's events.

She smiled and nodded, and, as if taking that as a cue to let loose, she asked. "What's in your hand?"

Jasyn almost forgot about the round object until she pointed it out.

He brought the object forward, resting it in his palm so she could see. She bent forward to look, but she was clearly confused. He couldn't blame her.

In his hand was a glass ball, a golden rim wrapping around it and a clasp at its center.

"It's my siblings' ashes. I bring them with me to all religious events so they can be bored with me." He laughed, but the joke must have not landed as intended, because Esi's eyes were sad.

"I'm so sorry for both of your losses."

It was as if the words were instinctual, as if she really blamed herself for his siblings' deaths, but... "You can stop apologizing." He shook his head. "It's a risk we take entering the Undertaking. Both of my siblings knew that."

"Do you miss them?" Her voice wavered at the question, as if she didn't feel like it was fair to ask.

"Daily, but I continue to live each day as best I can in their honor. I train for the Undertaking to continue our legacy."

"You marry me to strengthen the court."

"Exactly."

Esi twiddled her fingers. "Is that enough for you though?"

Jasyn was taken aback by the question—not because she shouldn't be asking, but because he never thought about it. So, he was honest.

"I spend every day feeling unworthy of the prospect of being king. Some days, I think I can do it and do it well, but days like yesterday...I doubt my abilities. I'm not the sociable, easy-to-speak-to person my siblings were. Yet, I keep trying, because I *want* to lead this court the best I can. Whether others want me to be their king is another question."

"I think you'll make a great king," Esi said.

"Even after I proved yesterday I can barely face my people?"

Esi rubbed her chin, as if truly pondering the question. He appreciated it; he needed honesty more than anything.

"Even then. We just might need to find ways to make it easier for you."

"Oh?"

"I have an idea," she said mischievously, and he wanted to kiss her right then, to lean forward and bring his lips to hers, taste her brilliance.

"Perhaps we will make a great couple then."

And she smiled, but for some reason, it didn't stretch her face like he hoped.

"King Jasyn and Queen Esi will be a perfect match, better than the Gods could have dreamed."

The way she said it felt like she was far removed from that statement, as if she was saying it from above instead of right here with him.

Eight

After Jasyn left to have lunch with his parents, Iskra sat idly in her room, with nothing to do for the rest of her day. She planned to go to him after, but Mych had informed her he wanted his alone time. The incident in the town square had still left him shaken, and he needed to re-energize. With such an early prayer service, he hadn't had a chance to follow his morning routine.

She wandered around the room at first, smelling the flowers Jasyn must have brought last night for Esi. A pang of jealousy coursed through her. She wished he had waited and given them to her. Then, she felt foolish. He didn't know there was a difference between the woman he knew during the day and the one at night.

Instead of pacing herself to the point of boredom, Iskra took Mych's offer to explore the glass castle. It was, as anticipated, large. It felt like the building never ended. When Bron noticed her leaving her room, he joined her. No doubt, he would rather be relaxing in his room, especially after that strange encounter with Kryth, but for optics, he needed to follow. Bron and Mych gave each other a knowing glance, like Mych understood the exact struggle of keeping watch of those of a higher rank. She wondered if the two of them had spoken after Mych escorted Kryth off the grounds.

The upstairs floor housed many rooms. Mych told her and Bron they were mostly unoccupied guest rooms, so they all made their way down. They took a spiral staircase into a green abyss. It was like a forest had been lifted from the ground and planted inside, or perhaps the castle had been built around it.

"I would think it would be dangerous to have so much flammable material inside one's home when those who occupy it have fire power," Iskra commented.

Bron stalled for a moment, and Iskra looked back at him, narrowing her eyes. He cleared his throat and continued, but Iskra didn't like the way he was acting. There was something he wasn't revealing, and it had to do with Kryth, the minister, since Bron didn't know Kryth's truth.

Mych shrugged. "It's not just Jasyn who feels connected to plants. They honor Slone and all the Weather Gods by giving them plants to sustain."

It was room after room of plants and fountains and ponds. In one room, there was a large pool. Iskra took off her silk shoes and dipped her toes in the water. It was cold, and small fish immediately rushed toward her, nibbling her feet.

What Iskra loved the most was that throughout their exploration of the castle, the sun always warmed her skin, unlike in the shop, where she was always shrouded in shadow.

"When will the king and queen return?"

Bron and Mych stopped whispering, and she almost felt guilty for disturbing them.

"Soon," Mych responded. "At least, that's my best guess. A party is scheduled in three days' time, and they never miss one."

"I'm sure they throw the most extravagant events," Iskra said almost longingly. She doubted she would be able to attend this party. Esi would step in for it, should the event take place at night.

"Extravagant and long. It will start as soon as the sun rises and end once it rises again the next day. Drinks, dancing, debauchery." He winked at Bron.

"Lady Esi will be on her best behavior," Bron stressed.

"And you?" Mych questioned.

"I will be on duty."

"That doesn't answer the question."

Iskra bit her bottom lip to keep the smile from crossing her face, but Bron seemed to notice it anyway and gave her a reprimanding look back.

Iskra linked her arms with Mych's. "I think you're a good influence."

"It's because someone needed to push Jasyn out of his comfort zone all these years. I'm glad you'll be taking the mantle now, though. It will give me time to focus on other things." Mych turned back to look at Bron, and Iskra snorted. Then, sadness took her by the throat as she tried to swallow down the reality she kept forgetting about. If all went how it was meant to, she would be dead in a few weeks.

Walking around the castle had exhausted her, so for the first time since she agreed to this mess, she allowed herself to lay in the large, four-poster bed. The silk sheets were so smooth, they felt like water on the skin, and the canopy curtains were luckily a soft-white and made of mesh netting, allowing her to see through them. It didn't feel like a cage when she enclosed herself. She fell asleep to the sounds of birds and windchimes.

She startled awake from the sound of voices in the hall. Shooting out of the bed, her face blanched. The sun was about to dip beyond the horizon. She would be shifting soon, and she needed to get in that cage before the castle had a very large problem.

Knocks sounded from the door, and she stilled.

"Who is it?"

"Me," Bron said, and he didn't bother getting her permission before he charged inside. "She's late."

Iskra knew he meant the real Esi. Iskra fumbled with her shoes before she headed to the balcony. She didn't have time to dawdle.

She was climbing down the sheets when Bron started coming down with her.

"What are you doing?" she hissed quietly, careful not to cause a raucous.

"Finding her."

"I'm sure she's heading this way," she reassured him. "Go back inside."

He didn't listen to her, and Iskra's stomach tightened. She needed to lose him before things went awry.

They were walking through an arched tunnel that led off the grounds when Iskra almost bumped into Esi. They both yelped in shock, but Esi recovered much faster than Iskra, who was breathing heavily from stress.

"Where were you?" Iskra seethed. "You should have been at the castle almost an hour ago."

Esi laughed. "Relax."

Iskra wanted to throttle the woman, but Bron stepped in before the tension could turn to violence. "We should head back before someone decides to knock on your door."

"Yes, please go," Iskra begged. She needed to leave. *Now*.

"What is all this worrying about?"

Iskra could smell alcohol on Esi's breath.

"You need to freshen up, too," Iskra warned, but Esi just giggled.

They were all so distracted by the conversation, they didn't hear the footsteps approaching them.

"And you need to get back to the shop before we cause a fright."

Iskra's heart stopped at Kryth's voice, more commanding and brutal in this form than the one he used as minister. When she turned to him, he held a cage. *Her* cage.

"Why do you act like she's a prisoner?" Esi asked brazenly. Her drunkenness was making her bold, and it would only get Iskra in trouble.

"She is mine," Kryth replied with such a lack of emotion, it made Iskra feel like she was nothing but a leaf in the wind.

"We should go," Iskra said to Kryth.

He shook his head. "We don't have time."

"Time for what?" Bron's voice was hard, his body going into defense mode. "And why do you have that cage?"

"Turn around," Iskra begged again, her voice wavering. "Please, go."

No amount of pleading would matter. She could feel a tingle starting at her burn mark; the scales wanted to claw their way out. Kryth opened the cage door, and she reached out.

"What's happening?" Esi hiccupped, but her tone was no longer loose and bright—it bubbled with concern.

"Our Iskra has had a great honor bestowed upon her," Kryth explained. "She will fight in the Undertaking."

"She wants to be queen?" Bron asked.

Kryth's smile was cold. "Worse. She will want to kill all the competitors."

Sun Court citizens didn't know the dragons in the Undertaking were actually shifters, humans in another form. But all the clues in front of him had Bron piecing it together. His face slackened as he volleyed his gaze between Iskra and Kryth.

"You're the minister." His eyes assessed Kryth closely, and Iskra could tell Bron saw it hidden beneath his current features. "How—"

But Iskra didn't have time to explain before her body shifted and entered the cage. The last glimpse she got was of Esi and Bron's shocked open mouths, their faces white with horror.

Nine

Jasyn was in a sour mood. He had told Mych he and Esi would head to whatever destination she had planned for them alone. His friend just laughed in his face. Bron's refusal had been extra vocal, an 'outrageous and dangerous idea,' as he put it.

As they all walked to town—a request made by Esi that he would never deny her—he noticed Bron more on edge than usual. Or, at least, his eyes never seemed to stray far from Esi for even a second. Of course, he wondered if there was any unrequited love there, but the way he looked at Esi was like she was a cannon ready to shoot at any moment, not someone he yearned for.

Luckily, the two guards gave them enough space to speak privately, likely Mych's doing. He would need to thank the man later.

"Do you ever get bored of the sun?" Esi asked as she leaned her head back, soaking in the light. He had his arm linked with hers to ensure she didn't bump into anything.

"You're like a sundrop," he replied, the words slipping from his mouth like oil.

She opened her eyes and gave him a quizzical look. Her eyes shone, the amber erring on the side of golden. He would never be able to look directly at the sun, but those damn eyes were like the sun rays themselves. More beautiful—and powerful too.

"And why's that?"

He tapped her nose, unable to help himself. "You blossom in the day but hide in the night."

He watched as her throat bobbed. He could tell she was forcing herself to keep his gaze. Hopefully, he didn't say something to offend her. He changed the subject for her sake.

"My parents' party is in two days. Can I count on your attendance?"

She didn't respond at first, and he started doubting every word he had uttered to her over the last few days. She hated him. She didn't want to marry him.

"Of course," she replied, but it wasn't enthusiastic. "You never answered my question, though."

She was redirecting their conversation, which, to be fair, he had done first.

"Well, Sundrop," he started, and he took in her content expression at the nickname as a good sign. "The sun is an extension of me. Do you get bored of your hands or your legs?"

She snorted, and the way her nose crinkled was the most beautiful sight. "No."

"I don't get bored of the sun, but I think it's because of all the opportunities I've had to get away from it. Visits to the Snow Court are common. I love going to the Lightning Court."

"It must be nice to have such power, to leave whenever you please."

"It is a privilege, yes."

Her face was now downcast, as if mulling over her sadness. He didn't like it. She deserved to shine with joy brighter than the sun.

"We're here." She stopped them, and Jasyn squinted as he read the sign.

"A bakery?"

The luscious smell coming from the shop reminded him of Dahlia. She'd had a sweet tooth, and she would always bring home fresh-baked delicacies. The memory of his sister made him smile sadly, but he allowed the grief its space and then let it go to live in the present with Esi.

"You like to use your hands," she said so quickly, the words must have not registered until she finished. Both of them blushed, but she cleared her throat. "I figured we could bake something and distribute it to the children in the square."

He knew it was foolish, that it had only been days, but he was starting to fall for the woman in front of him. She was fiery yet so kind and understanding. She saw him so deeply, he wondered if she could read his mind.

Yet, a frightening question popped up as they entered the bakery: what if she didn't reciprocate those feelings? Right now, he ignored that thought.

"Lead the way, Sundrop."

Iskra knew, with every passing day, she was digging herself into a deeper hole. Her secrets were unraveling, and the way Bron had his eyes on her felt like she had a target on her back. She knew as soon as they had a private moment, he would be livid with her. Perhaps he would even cancel Iskra and Esi's scheme. It would be for the best, because being around Jasyn was dangerous. He had some hold on her, like an invisible rope around her body. She needed to sever it before he reined her in fully.

This is temporary, she reminded herself as they entered the bakery.

Chocolate and sugar and fresh baked bread coated her senses. There was a glass case filled with various pastries and desserts—colorful cookies, sugared decorations, intricate chocolate designs. A three tiered cake in the corner mocked her, a reminder that a wedding was not on the table for her.

"Prince Jasyn." The head baker bowed his head. "Lady Esi, lovely to see you again." He smiled at her.

She had visited the bakery right when it opened this morning, asking the baker if she and Jasyn could come and bake something together. After she explained who exactly she was, he'd obliged her request.

Jasyn leaned forward, closely inspecting the desserts. His green eyes took in every detail. He reached out toward the more intricately decorated cakes, but he was hindered by the glass encasement keeping them safe.

"Such skill," Jasyn whispered to himself, but Iskra and the baker glanced at each other, smiling at his words.

"The first step is to bake, and then you can attempt to decorate."

Jasyn turned to the two of them. Mych and Bron stayed outside, protecting the exterior and keeping everyone out.

"I have no such skill, but I will try nonetheless."

Iskra wondered if that was Jasyn's philosophy on becoming king, on life in general. He would always try, even with the possibility of failure.

"Join me in the back," the baker told them both.

They followed him behind the counter into the back room, where a blast of heat hit them.

"Instructions are here for anything you wish to bake." The baker pointed to a book. "Ingredients can be found in the cabinets. I'll be in the front."

"You're not helping us?" Iskra asked.

He gave them a playful smile. "I think this a perfect test of compatibility, how well the two of you can work together on something you have no knowledge on."

The baker left them both then, closing the door behind him.

Iskra's mouth hung open, and then she huffed a laugh. "I promise, I thought he would guide us through it."

Jasyn shrugged, already flipping through the pages of the recipe book. "It's an exciting challenge."

Iskra cringed. "One the castle will need to pay for."

Jasyn paused and looked up to her. She thought he was about to scold her, but his eyes shimmered with delight. "I would expect nothing less."

His eyes strayed back to the book, and she allowed him to decide what they should make.

"How about these fruit rolls with a simple vanilla glaze? They were my sister's favorite."

There was so much emotion crossing Jasyn's face in that one moment. She was determined to make it work. They could do this small thing to bring Jasyn close to his sister again.

Iskra eyed the recipe, and she had no idea if it was of advanced skill. She knew nothing about the art of cooking and baking. She knew nothing much of the world, she supposed. Being locked in a cage as a dragon didn't allow her the opportunity to experience much. What little life she had before was secluded.

"There's an assortment of berries that would be perfect," she said as she pointed behind them to a basket filled with freshly picked berries.

However, instead of looking at them, Jasyn had his eyes on her. She had leaned over him when she scanned the page, and now, they both were at eye level. Her breathing hitched as his eyes narrowed down to her mouth. She bit her bottom lip, and a guttural groan escaped him, as if he was forcing himself back, that rope pulled tighter and tighter.

"We should—" She swallowed.

"Bake," he finished for her.

She nodded. "Before the baker wonders what's taking so long. It'll be dark if we keep stalling, and all the children will be back home for dinner."

Jasyn nodded along, yet they both stayed in the same position. Neither was willing to pull back first.

"I would like to spend the night with you." The words were out of his mouth fast, but he backed away quicker. He rubbed at the back of his neck. "That was inappropriate. Apologies, Lady Esi."

Iskra now stood at the table while he leaned against the counter, chest heaving.

"No apologies needed. Should we begin?"

"You still want to do this?"

"Bake?" she asked.

"Get married." His voice cracked.

Iskra was taken aback. There was so much doubt in those few words, regret and fear and *longing*.

Worst of all, she couldn't respond as herself. It was Lady Esi who said, "Of course, I still want to marry you. Why would you think otherwise?"

"There is something about you that confuses me," he said so sincerely, it broke her.

What she did next, she would excuse as an act of comfort required to keep the betrothal strong. It wasn't like her to initiate contact like this, but she refused to be the cause of the end.

Slowly, she stepped closer to him, each step punctuated with the racing of her heart. She took his cheek in her hand, and at first, he didn't respond. Then, he rested comfortably against her palm. Iskra had to hold back tears at how *right* it felt, how simple it was to be with this man.

"There will be no doubts."

She went up to her toes and pressed a soft kiss to his lips. Once again, he didn't respond at first, but as she went to pull away, he wrapped his arm around her waist, keeping her in against him. She had to place her hand on his chest to avoid fully falling into him. Now, his lips moved against hers, slow, sensual, yearning in his touch. She felt it all. He didn't rush them, even when she opened her mouth to let him in. No, he kept it demure. It didn't stop the rush of desire pooling at her core, though, and she wanted to rub her thighs together to satiate herself.

Instead, he pulled back and rested his forehead against hers. "We should bake."

She was left breathless as he stepped out of their embrace and started collecting everything they needed for the rolls.

Ten

Their pastries tasted better than they looked. Thankfully, as long as sugar was involved, children didn't care about appearances.

Jasyn and Esi had four large baskets filled to the brim with goodies. Mych and Bron helped lug them as they distributed items to the children and families. As soon as the children saw them coming, they stopped their games and sprinted over.

Jasyn was now down on one knee, smiling so much, his cheeks had begun to ache. The children said their thank yous but didn't bow or treat him like a prince. He was just another person to them.

Throughout the whole afternoon, Esi was at his side. She constantly checked on him without even using a word, her eyes communicating her concern and comfort, soothing him.

Even when there was a gaggle of children, Jasyn remained calm. He breathed through it and distracted himself with passing out more of the rolls. Esi had been right. He was most at ease when he was preoccupied with doing something.

It made conversations with adults easier too. And when he began to feel a rush of panic, Esi was there to take his place. She spoke about the beauty of this court and the royal family, how generous and kind they had been in the short time she had been staying with them. What stood out most of all: she expressed her excitement about seeing Jasyn thrive in the Undertaking and marrying him.

Though the kiss was reassurance enough that their feelings were mutual, her words were an added layer.

When everyone had their treats, Jasyn packed up a few for his parents, who were returning tonight, just in time for their party in two days' time.

Esi came up to him, and he could see how relaxed she appeared.

"I think this was successful."

"Very." He nodded. "I have you to thank." He wiped at her cheek where there was a small smattering of glaze. He brought his finger to his mouth and licked it clean. He loved the way her eyes followed his movements.

She cleared her throat. "I am told I must head to the seamstress, a final fitting for my dress for the party."

"You're not coming back?" He hated how weak he sounded.

"I'll be back," she promised. "By tomorrow morning, I'll be back."

He kicked a pebble around. "I never asked if you would be my honored guest at the party."

"I didn't realize there was a choice."

"You value freedom," he said sincerely. "Of course you can make a choice."

She didn't hesitate as she replied, "I'll be your honored guest."

There was so much relief that came with her statement. Even in this short time together, he couldn't remember his life without her. She completed him in a way he didn't realize.

"Then I should let you go to make sure you have something to wear."

She inched closer and pressed a swift kiss to his cheek. "Good night, Jasyn. Today was lovely."

Then, she was running off with her guard. He was mesmerized at how breathtaking she was, silhouetted against the setting sun. He wished he could follow her.

When she was far enough away, Jasyn lightly stroked his cheek. As he turned around, Mych clapped and whistled.

"Look at you go," he teased. "Winning over her heart so quickly."

"Don't be an ass."

"I'm being sincere." Mych bumped his shoulder against Jasyn's. "You both look happy. I feared you would never allow yourself to open up to someone, with the amount of death you've faced."

"Are *you* happy?" Jasyn asked, wanting to turn the subject away from him. There were times Jasyn thought that, just like him, Mych was lonely. He had left his family right as he turned eighteen to join the royal guard. As the youngest member, he had been at the bottom of the hierarchy, but he had quickly moved up the ranks to Jasyn's personal one because of his compassion. During one of

Jasyn's panicked moments, Mych had been there to bring him down with care.

"I would be happier if Bron wasn't a stubborn brat."

"Oh? Why do you say that?"

The two started trekking back to the castle. It had been a long day, and Jasyn's back ached, but he wouldn't trade the pain for the sun itself. It meant he had filled his day with Esi.

"I think Bron holds some affection for Lady Esi."

"I had come to the same conclusion." Jasyn sighed, unsure of what that meant for him and Esi. Did she and Bron ever act on anything before? It wouldn't matter to him what she did in the past, but…did any feelings linger?

"It's going to make working together once you're both married very complicated." Mych snapped Jasyn out of his unraveling doubt.

"What's your solution?"

"Turn that affection in my direction."

Jasyn stopped in his tracks. "You're joking."

"Of course not, Jasyn. It's the perfect solution. I'm attractive. He's attractive. We would make the most attractive couple, even beating the future king and queen."

Jasyn threw his head back and laughed. "Perhaps you're right. Bron could use someone as easygoing as you."

"Because he always acts like there is a stick up his ass?"

"Exactly."

They neared the castle, and he saw a carriage parked there. His parents.

A guard was lifting his father into his wheelchair when they reached them. His mother was right behind him, a warm smile on her face. Jasyn wondered if his mother was relieved now that his father would no longer be putting himself in danger, though those fears were shifted towards Jasyn, no doubt. He wished his mother could live without that burden weighing her.

"You're home," Jasyn said as he wrapped his arms around his mother, holding her extra tight. He passed over the basket with the rolls, and his mother immediately took a bite with a satisfied sigh.

"Jasyn is in love," Mych said cheekily.

His parents snapped their attention to him.

"Truly?" his father's gruff voice asked as he rolled up closer. "I knew you two would be a power match, but it is a gift from Slone if it's a love match too."

"Lady Esi is caring. She has taught me things about myself I didn't even know," Jasyn said.

"You *are* in love," his mother said, her excitement palpable as she squeezed his shoulders. Her dark curls were adorned with gold decorations that framed her face beautifully.

"We should pop open a bottle of sparkling wine," his father announced.

"Let's not celebrate too early. I have an Undertaking to get through first."

"Even more of a reason to open the alcohol," Mych muttered under his breath as they entered the glass castle.

The appointment with the seamstress wasn't for another hour, but the way Bron yanked her onward, one would think they were running late. The lively streets were busy with townspeople decorating for the party. Flags and ribbons hung from tree branches; flower beds in front of windows were being watered. Children ran around with chalk in their hands, coloring the streets with their drawings. It made Iskra smile, but that quickly disappeared.

"You have explaining to do," Bron huffed. "You and that owner of yours, Kryth." He said the minister's name like it was a curse.

"He's not my owner." The words were fruitless. No matter how much she wished they were true, they weren't.

"He's the minister, and you're nothing but his pet."

Iskra flinched at the words, like they were a blow to the gut.

They were at the shop, and this time, Bron went in through the back, Iskra right behind him. Esi was studying the cages closely, reaching toward the other dragons. They nipped at her finger, and instead of swiping her hand away, she laughed lightly.

"That tickles," she said quietly. Kryth raised a brow at her and shook his head. She was an enigma, but she turned to Bron and asked, "Why did you bring us all here?"

"Start explaining," Bron ordered both Kryth and Iskra.

Kryth snorted. His appearance was as the minister, and Iskra thought she hated that more than his shop owner form. Iskra crossed her arms, her eyes on the empty cage.

Esi slapped her guard gently on his shoulder.

"Don't be rude," Esi chastised. "We still need them."

Everyone in the room stilled.

Esi eyed each of them but stopped on Iskra. "This isn't over just because you transform into a dragon."

"How about that she lied to us? Not just about her being a dragon, but about Jasyn," Bron pushed.

Although Iskra's eyes were entirely focused on the two bickering, she could feel Kryth's stern gaze on her. She heard the sizzle of fire, and then the air began to fill with smoke. Kryth didn't say anything as he smoked from his pipe, as if waiting to see how this conversation would turn without his input.

"It was an omission of truth," Esi reasoned as she braided her hair and tied it with a white ribbon.

"What have you learned that had to remain such a secret?" Kryth asked.

"Nothing," Iskra snapped.

"His power," Esi replied.

"His light," Bron corrected.

Kryth bounced his attention between the three of them then took another puff. As he blew out the smoke, he looked at Iskra.

"An interesting revelation. He should be an easy kill if he has no flame."

"How does that work?" Esi asked. "I mean, don't dragons have fire within them? So how does fire kill them?"

"He doesn't mean an easy kill for me," Iskra explained. "He will be easily killed by the others competing. The only way to kill a dragon is to pierce their heart."

Esi furrowed her brows, as if Iskra's destiny finally occurred to her. "Meaning he will be killing you... I had no idea the dragons were shifters this whole time."

Iskra shrugged. No one did, but her whole existence had been leading to that moment. "We should discuss if we still plan to move forward with all this." Iskra gestured at the air between them.

"Yes." Esi nodded.

"No," Bron urged, his arms extended toward Esi, as if he wanted to shake her. "No, Esi. It's too dangerous. You should be the one at the party anyways."

"I don't want to lose any time with Dominik," Esi pleaded.

"He's right," Iskra jumped in. "You should be at the party. It goes through the night, and I can't be there during that."

"Not even once?" That question was directed to Kryth. "You clearly have some magic within those bottles you house in front of your shop to transform yourself as you please."

Kryth coughed into his arm. "Why would I allow that?"

"So there is a way?" Esi's voice had pitched with excitement.

"I ask again: why would I do that?"

"Because the Gods love a show."

Kryth laughed through his nose, and the sound made goosebumps rise on Iskra's skin.

"That is true," Kryth said. "They have shown me in my dreams that they have been delighting in the drama we've orchestrated."

Iskra didn't fail to notice that whenever Kryth spoke, Bron averted his gaze.

"See?" Esi said.

"One night," Kryth warned.

Iskra whipped her gaze to Kryth. "How?"

But her question was drowned out by Esi's cheers and claps. Bron looked like he wanted to chew Kryth's head off.

"Oh, you'll have the loveliest time. And the dress? Jasyn will fall to his knees," Esi chirped. Esi linked her arm with Bron's, and they began heading to the door.

Iskra turned to Kryth and repeated her question. "How?"

"The Gods work in mysterious ways. Just like I could change your hair and my own appearance, I could temporarily pause your shifting for a night. I don't recommend doing it often, since it is painful, and it forces one to seek relaxing effects from other addictive ways," Kryth puffed his pipe to exaggerate. "But you'll be dead in a few weeks anyways."

Emotions rushed through the surface. Iskra would have a night with Jasyn. She couldn't believe it. Her body began to flame at just the thought of them being together for that long. And then she remembered—she wasn't actually his bride. Esi was.

Iskra ran out the shop, thankful Kryth hadn't stopped her, though the bluing sky indicated her time was limited.

"Esi!" she called, and the lady stopped and turned.

She let go of Bron, but he didn't stray far.

"I—thank you. I'm sorry for all the lies."

Esi grabbed her shoulder. "No apologies needed. I get to spend a night with Dominik."

"You love him?" Iskra asked.

"Very much," she responded, and there was sadness in her eyes. "I would give it all up to be with him, but I understand my responsibility to the court."

"How did you know you loved him?"

Esi smiled, and it was the most beautiful thing. "Love isn't complicated. It was a sensation in my chest at first. Then, it was the realization of how much I would risk to spend any second I could with him. It was taking that chance with you to continue fostering that love until our time ran out. It was understanding that the best thing I can do once I marry Jasyn is to let Dominik go so he could find love again, even if it wasn't with me."

Iskra wiped the tears in her eyes. "I kissed him," she admitted.

"Jasyn?" Esi asked, so simply, so nonchalantly.

Iskra nodded. "I'm sorry. I understand if that is too far and you change your mind."

But Esi shook her head. "You deserve to experience that all-consuming love too. Fuck him if you must."

Iskra opened and closed her mouth at the vulgarity. "Are you not mad?"

"Honestly, I pity you. You have spent your life locked up with no opportunity to *feel*. Take this opportunity, grasp it, let it squeeze every emotion from your heart." Esi tightened her hand to a fist. "Jasyn and I will never be a love-match. Plus, I'm not being so innocent right now either." Her eyes twinkled, and Iskra looked over Esi's shoulders to where Bron's eyes were downcast.

"I don't know if we'll go that far, but it has been one of the most freeing sensations to fall for this man. I appreciate you giving this to me."

Esi winked. "Women are not meant for cages. We are meant to soar."

Eleven

Jasyn fidgeted with the cuffs of his sleeves. It was a mesh fabric, hand-sewn with beads in the shape of flowers. It let the warm breeze through, and although most days, he would feel shy, today was the perfect occasion for such an ostentatious garment.

The yearly party thrown by the royal family was a celebration for all, a time to let loose before the possibility that, a few weeks later, the court could burn to the ground.

It was also a way for the royal family to experience the extravagance of royalty one last time in case the competing royal lost and a new person took over. His parents did not hold back. The castle workers spent days cleaning every glass surface, scrubbing the stone floors, and decorating every inch of the grounds.

Jasyn tried not thinking about that aspect of it, how in a few short days, this castle might no longer be his home. It's all he knew, and saying goodbye would break him. Instead of chasing those thoughts, he was standing on the bottom of the stairs like a dog, waiting for Esi to appear. It would be a long day and night, and he couldn't wait to spend it with her.

"Don't be nervous," Mych teased.

"Shouldn't you be wooing Bron?" Jasyn snapped back, and his guard shook his head as he laughed.

"The wooing will commence as soon as you and Esi are at each other's hips."

"What does that mean?"

"It means...it's like pulling a stubborn weed from the dirt when it comes to separating you two."

Jasyn scoffed. "That's ridiculous."

"But true."

Jasyn was ready to fight the notion further, but footsteps sounded on the stone stairs.

Esi gripped the railing tightly, but he barely noticed her wobbling. She was a vision before him. She wore a long ivory silk dress, her train sweeping behind her. It had short, fluttering sleeves that bounced as she moved. It would have been shapeless, save for the porcelain corset at her waist. It had a marbled effect of reds, oranges, and yellows, a picture of the sun up close. Her hair was down in waves, embellished with clips that looked like the ruby gemstone of the Heart.

"Close your mouth," were Mych's parting words.

Jasyn shook himself out of the fog. "You look...breathtaking." Breathtaking wasn't enough to describe Esi's beauty. She radiated, and he could do nothing but stare in awe.

She played with the beading on his sleeves. "You look handsome."

Now that she was before him, he noticed how her cheeks were rosy, her eyes covered in an iridescent glitter.

When she caught him staring, she said, "Your mother told me the more shine, the better."

"She was right."

"I tried refusing the shoes, but she told me it was necessary—for the daytime, at least. At night is when the party truly unfolds, and I can whip them off." Esi lifted the skirt of the dress to reveal strappy shoes so high, it was no wonder she was struggling.

"I'll make sure to not let you fall." He extended his arm, and he saw relief wash over her face.

She stepped cautiously off the final stair, and they were together at the hip like Mych had proclaimed. Jasyn chuckled to himself.

The festivities had started at sunrise, music and cheering everywhere. People were already dancing and drinking in the ballroom, but Jasyn guided Esi to the throne room.

"Unfortunately, the first part of the day requires us to be responsible."

"How so?"

"Greeting guests." Esi shuddered, and he knocked his shoulder against hers. "It won't be that bad."

The throne room was crowded with everyone wanting to give their hellos to the royal family. With Esi on his arm, it was easy to move through the chaos. He carefully guided her over the stone steps of the pond, carrying the end of her dress, making sure she could skip across them without falling into the water.

His parents were just as extravagantly dressed. His father wore a sleeveless silk shirt that showed off his muscled arms, and his mother looked refined in her maroon dress.

"You make such a beautiful couple." His mother smiled, and he blushed at the attention.

"I have you to thank for my appearance, although I'm not surprised you were right. The glitter was a requirement."

"See?" His mother patted her husband's arm, which rested on his throne. "I am always right."

His father leaned in as close to his mother as he could, and she inched her face in to accept the kiss. "I never doubted you."

Before he met Esi, he would have turned away from such a display of affection. He thought that love would never find him. He thought he didn't deserve it, but Esi changed that for him.

"Go have fun," his father said. "No need to worry about royal duties this year. You'll have decades of it soon enough."

Jasyn nodded, resenting the confidence. He hoped he had the responsibility in his future. He *wanted* it, but desire did not guarantee him the throne.

As they moved away from the dais, Esi leaned in. "He's right. You'll be on that throne next year."

Jasyn gave her a half-hearted smile, but he didn't want to think about the future right now. He only wanted to experience the present with the woman in his arms.

"Let's dance," he said.

Iskra's feet and calves burned. The shoes were a nuisance, and when Jasyn could no longer take her wincing in pain, he sat her down and slowly lifted the skirt of her dress, lingering on her calves before he undid the clasp of her shoes. She moaned in relief, but he held on to her leg and pressed a kiss to her shin. Goosebumps dotted her skin, and he only smirked up at her when he saw her body react.

"You're beautiful." His voice was sensual and soft, and it hit something deep at the apex of her thighs.

"You've told me that three times already." He wouldn't stop saying it as they danced together. Each time, it made her face heat even more.

"It's true." He shrugged as he released the skirts from his grasp and sat in the chair opposite hers.

The whole ballroom was surrounded by brass tables and chairs, and the perimeter was alight with fire. Candles covered every empty spot, and when Iskra asked if that was a fire risk, he told her the fire was magic. It wouldn't burn anything as long as whoever lit it kept it in its place. When Iskra anchored her head upwards, she was rewarded with a view of colorful ribbons hanging across the glass ceiling. At the end of them were small glass orbs that caught the sunlight pouring in, glowing across the whole room.

Yet, it was watching others enjoying themselves that warmed her heart. Everyone was dressed spectacularly in their finest, shiniest garments. Some wore masks, which Jasyn informed her was a way to keep one's identity safe as they let the debauchery of the night consume them.

One of the servants passed by with a tray of sparkling wine, and Jasyn swiped two flutes. He handed one over to her, and they clinked the crystal glasses.

"To us and our bright future."

Iskra sipped and swallowed both the drink and the growing lump in her throat. This sparkling day would be one of the best in her life. When Jasyn had a sword at her heart during the Undertaking, this would be the memory she would come back to as the light left her eyes.

"What's wrong?"

Iskra snapped her head to Jasyn, who had put down the glass and leaned over the table towards her.

She smiled. "Show me your favorite place."

He smiled back at her and took her hand. They ran out, neither of them caring if anyone stared at them when they left the castle to the sounds of chirping bugs. Iskra turned around to glance at the building, and it truly was a marvel. She could see all the candles inside, the building seeming like it was burning.

Jasyn pulled on her arm, and they were off again.

They slowed, and when Jasyn faced her, she could read the nerves on her face. "It's not anything original, but this garden is unlike the rest. I never touch it. I let everything grow as Slone intends."

"Why does this one remain unchanged?" she asked, her heart beating rapidly.

"This was the garden my siblings and I would spend hours playing in as children. It's the one place that will keep growing without change, even when they are gone. Even when I'm gone."

Iskra wiped the tear rolling down his face with her thumb. "That's beautiful." Her hand trailed to his chest, where she felt the rushing rhythm of his heartbeat. "Your soul is beautiful, Jasyn. You'll make such a wonderful king."

"I hope my people feel the same way."

She snapped her gaze to his, taking in his green eyes filled with so much doubt. She hated the sight of it.

"The people already love you. You might not be your siblings, but you're *you*. A man with a kind heart who wants good things for this court. A man with a unique gift from Slone, one you shouldn't be afraid to shine in front of others just because it's not the harsh heat of flame."

He nodded, but she had a feeling the words didn't stick fully. She wished he could believe her, but she knew he ultimately had to accept the words as truth himself.

"I want to share this with you..." He gestured towards the reason they were here.

He opened the latch of a white wooden fence, and it was like stepping inside a dream. They were surrounded by a burst of colors. The grass reached Iskra's knees, and she could hear the trickling of water somewhere to her left.

"It's so..." No words could encompass the sensation she felt as she stepped into this other world, but she finally landed on one. "Peaceful."

She laughed at herself; that barely brimmed the surface of it. Jasyn was right in front of her now, clasping her chin so it was tilted toward him.

"Your laugh is my undoing. I want to swallow it until it's embedded in my soul."

"Do it," she said brazenly. Her entire body scorched with the eternal flame of her desire for him.

He leaned down and kissed her, and she laughed into his mouth. This time, he didn't hold back. His tongue swiped into her mouth, and she moaned as she gripped his hips to bring him closer. They both wore such thin fabric, she could feel his hardness against her.

It was overwhelming, how one person could make her feel so much with such little touch. Her body had been craving this her whole life, and she had been denied such an experience before this. Once this moment was over, she would grieve the lost potential of so many years she'd been stuck in a cage.

Before she could tell what was happening, he undid the ties at the back of her corset. It dropped to the ground with a thud, but she didn't care, because Jasyn was now gripping her waist tightly, and she delighted in how firm his grip was, like she was his anchor keeping him from floating away.

"Is this okay?" he asked, as his lips moved to a spot behind her ears.

Even in a state of such desire, he was a gentleman. It made her eyes burn. Esi would be such a lucky wife.

Before she could respond, he lifted her to bring her gently down into the grass. The sky was a burning mixture of reds and oranges, but darkness would sweep over them soon. For the first time since she had been captured by Kryth, she would experience the night sky.

His mouth was on her clavicle, and she arched into him as he rolled his hips into her core. She whimpered at how *good* it felt.

"Is this okay?" he repeated.

It was hard to answer as his hand began pulling the sleeves of her dress off her shoulders. Soon, the dress would be down her navel, and he would see the brand on the underside of her breast.

"I've never done this—" she practically shouted.

He kissed her shoulder softly and looked at her for a moment. "Me neither."

That alone was a splash of cold water. She couldn't be doing this with him. He deserved to know the person he was giving his body to for the first time, not some lie dressed as a fraud.

She got up on her elbows, and his brows frowned. He rolled off her, though, sensing her distress.

"Maybe we should wait." Her voice shook, because, deep down, she wanted him. She wanted to entwine their bodies and souls, but she couldn't, not even if Esi had given her permission.

Jasyn recovered quickly. He hopped onto his feet and extended his hands toward her. He always had his arms waiting for her. She took them and got to her feet as well. He grabbed the corset, but she shook her head.

"I think I want to dance the night away comfortably. With you," she added to stress how much she wanted him, that she wasn't pushing him away.

"You lead, and I will always follow."

She wished that was true, but not too long from now, he would not be able to follow her in death. Luckily, he would never know the difference between her and Esi. Their connection would be extinguished by the Undertaking, just like her existence.

Twelve

Days passed, and Iskra barely had any alone time with Jasyn. Since his parents returned, Jasyn had been focused on spending time with them and, more importantly, training. Though, every meal, the full royal family ate together, and she was invited. It was always a casual affair, but the King and Queen spoke about their past—how they met, how they ruled, bestowing crumbs of advice on the future couple. Iskra did her best not to look at Jasyn too long, because she feared she would crumble. She would never get to see Jasyn crowned.

King Aleks also told her how he had ended up in the wheelchair. Dahlia had been fighting her way through the Undertaking, her father at her back, protecting her. While she was busy engaging with another competitor who wanted to kill her, King Aleks didn't notice the dragon at his back. It had swiped its tail so forcefully, the king flew across the cave and hit a rock right on his spine. He had been unable to walk since. Dahlia had witnessed it, and, instead of focusing on the Undertaking, she tried helping him. As she had kneeled in front of her father, he yelled a warning, but it was too late. A sword plunged through her chest.

King Aleks only came out victorious because another competitor practically handed him the Heart. He had been a strong supporter of the king, and he wanted his reign to continue. It wasn't a rare occurrence for Sun Court citizens to enter with the goal of ensuring a certain outcome. If the participant survived, King Aleks would honor and reward them to show his gratitude. Yet, even that hadn't been enough to see Jaymes or Dahlia on the throne.

Iskra took the story in stride, but the truth of the matter was, she felt responsible. It was her kind that had been killing and hurting people. Soon, she would be the one to end a life. That sinking reality stuck with her as she headed to the shop for the night, except instead of the usual quiet streets, she was greeted with the sight of Bron handing Kryth a small satchel.

She stayed back, watching the exchange for a moment. They spoke in hushed tones, but their faces revealed the brimming tension between them.

Iskra stepped forward, her curiosity reaching a peak. "What's happening?"

Both whipped their attention to her. Bron practically jumped in shock, but Kryth remained nonchalant, already having been tuned to her presence from afar.

Kryth smiled as he tossed the satchel, metal loudly clattering in her ear. There was money in there.

Iskra volleyed her gaze between the two men, unable to put together any situation in which Bron owed Kryth money. Had he bought something from the shop?

Kryth seemed eager to quench her growing list of questions. "He did everything he could to try and save Siena. His biggest mistake was coming to me."

"You lied to me!" Bron yelled, his voice impassioned. "You said you could save her."

"I don't understand." Iskra shook her head. "You went to Kryth to buy something from him to save your mother?"

"I went to the minister, as I was told he had familiarity with herbal medicines that could heal any ailment. As the minister, I figured he would be the best. Back then, he had a different location, somewhere closer to where I grew up. Now, it all makes sense. He's a liar and a fraud, in more ways than one." Bron gestured to the shop in front of them.

Kryth smiled. "And he couldn't pay up then, so he owes me now. I heard you've had to go to reckless measures to get the coin for all the medicines I concocted for you."

Iskra's face blanched. "What did you do?"

Bron's face was downcast. "I've been gambling to make up the money, but I'm still in so much debt for the years of trying to keep her alive." Bron pointed to Kryth. "You don't deserve one coin of it."

It all made sense then, *why* Bron seemed annoyed by the betrothal between Esi and Jasyn. It wasn't that he held affection for the lady.

He must have wanted to marry her for the money. Iskra couldn't dive deeper into the situation, though, because Kryth's next words hit Iskra and Bron like a ball of fire.

"Why would I have wanted to save my sister after she spent my whole life discouraging me from taking the title of minister?"

Jasyn sprung from his bed early. Ever since the party, he'd felt like he was flying. He and Esi were a love-match. She craved him as much as he craved her. Even when she stopped them from taking that next step, he still felt their connection. It showed she trusted him enough to voice her truth. It was like a fire lit within him when he decided he would go to town this morning. Alone.

Well...almost alone.

Mych trailed Jasyn as they neared the town square. It was an unusually cloudy day, but Jasyn enjoyed the break from the scorching heat.

"Are you sure?" Mych asked.

"I answered yes three times. My mind won't change."

It was early enough that it was still quiet. There were children outside, but they were tired and moved slowly. Mothers had to herd them along, a warming sight. They carried baskets or pulled barrows filled with clothes. It was washing day, and Jasyn planned to help.

A river slithered not too far away, and he followed along. Townsfolk gave him curious glares, but he offered to carry a basket from a nearby woman. She hesitated, but he urged her. Then, he made Mych do the same.

At the river, he watched as the mothers began washing the clothes in the water, showing their children how it was done. Some of the unfocused ones just jumped into the current and splashed each other.

He wanted to join them, but he kept to the task. He noted how the women were scrubbing the fabrics against each other to remove stains, some even using a smooth rock to massage the clothes.

A woman noticed him. "Are you here to learn, Prince Jasyn?"

"And help," he added.

"This work is below you. I—we—" she gestured around, "wouldn't feel uncomfortable allowing you to get on your knees."

He wanted to push, but it was unfair. He would disrupt their rhythm. Still, he looked at how they hung the clothes on branches or laid them on rocks, how many of the women commented on how long it would take the clothes to dry with the lack of sun, and an idea formed. Esi's words from the party rang through him. She was right. He shouldn't hide his gift from his people. There shouldn't be secrets, and even if his light wasn't as magnificent as before his siblings' deaths, it was still powerful.

Moving to the clothes, he called to his light and let the warmth exuding from his hands dry the fabrics quickly. Eyes were on him, but he didn't mind. He was in control of the situation, of his mind and body.

"Magic!" a child yelled, and he heard their footsteps pounding against the pebbles.

Where one went, the others followed. Soon, he had a herd of them surrounding him.

"Me next! Me next!" A young girl bounced on her small feet as she lifted the end of her dress toward him.

Jasyn chuckled and gently let his light glow against the dress. The children watched in awe as the fabric lightened before their eyes.

With that one trick, all the children started hounding him to dry their clothes next. It was chaotic and overwhelming, but he reminded himself of the world before him—the ground beneath his feet, the stream of water in the river, the sounds of birds and families around him.

When he had dried the fifth child, he swore his eyes were playing tricks as Esi appeared from behind the trees and waved at him, her face like a gentle breeze on a hot day.

Yet, for some odd reason, his response was to panic.

He smiled at the children before jogging off toward her. Mych was not too far behind, keeping a close eye on them both.

"What are you doing here?" She should be at the castle. "Did you come here alone?"

Esi blinked and crossed her arms.

"I didn't realize I was a prisoner."

Her words were sharp, and they hit him hard. Yet, it didn't quell that rising tide of fear. She shouldn't be out here alone.

"You could be killed," he snapped.

"By whom? The children?" She scoffed.

"We should go," Mych urged. "You have an audience."

Jasyn turned around, and everyone seemed to snap their attention away as soon as he did. The young girl—the first to have her clothes dried—came up to them with flowers tied together to form a crown. She reached up to give it to Esi, who bent down to be at the same height as the child. She placed it on Esi's head, and some of the panic began to wash away, like dirt scrubbed from clothes.

"You're pretty," the young girl said, her voice giggly.

Esi tapped the child's nose. "You look like a princess in your dress."

The girl giggled again, and like all children, something else quickly caught her attention, causing her to rush off.

Before they could leave, though, one of the mothers approached them.

"Thank you, Prince Jasyn, for your kindness."

Jasyn opened his mouth to stop the undeserved praise, but her next statement made him stop.

"You'll make a great king." She winked before nodding to Esi and Mych and then leaving. He held in his breath, unable to let the words worm their way in. He'd simply offered a helping hand today.

Even though Esi clearly was angry with him, she touched his cheek like she understood the effect those words had on him, how he had difficulty accepting them.

"Let's go," she whispered.

Thirteen

"Somewhere private," Iskra requested. As Jasyn guided her, she felt the vibrations of his body. What had overcome him? He was moving quickly, and she could sense them losing Mych. Iskra didn't think it was because the guard couldn't keep up. She guessed he wanted to give the future married couple some space.

Their steps sounded on the stone floors of the castle, and she had to duck to avoid being slapped by leaves, branches extending towards them like eager arms.

"The throne room?" She raised one of her brows.

"No one goes in there unless we have official business."

She sighed. It would have to do. She pressed her finger to his chest. "Just us. Make sure no one comes in."

He didn't hesitate as he reached up to a sconce right next to the door and revealed a key. Without stumbling a beat, he locked the door to the throne room, and Iskra could *feel* the difference of that simple action. One second, they were two people together in a room, and the next, they were two people with the freedom to exist together without fear of disruption.

Iskra craned her neck up. She still wasn't used to the sight of it, the way the arched, vaulted ceilings touched so high in the sky. The plants consumed the room, making it feel like they had an audience, but it was just them, hidden within the greenery.

"What happened out there?" she asked, her voice wavering. A part of her thought she had no right to push him like this. He was a prince. She was a nobody.

Jasyn wasn't looking at her when he responded. "You could have died."

"By whose hands?"

He whipped around away from the door, his hands up in frustration as he accentuated each word. "That's not the point."

"Why are you so scared?"

"Because I have lost so much, and I can't lose you too!"

His chest heaved deeply, the pupils of those green eyes shot wide. Iskra stood there stunned. No words would form; no thoughts eddied in her mind.

"I have lost and lost. I cannot fathom a world without you in it, and that terrifies me."

And again, no words would leave her mouth. She didn't have them. How could she comfort him with lies? She would be gone. He would lose the person he had become acquainted with during the day and only have the Esi of the night. He would win the Undertaking—she would do everything in her power to guarantee it—and he would marry someone else.

It was grieving any potential of them together that pushed her off the ledge she had been tiptoeing on for days. Perhaps words were not needed right now.

"Sit," she ordered as she pointed to his father's throne.

She watched Jasyn's throat bob, but he followed her lead, walking the stone path across the pond with ease. Even with her shoes off, Iskra's own adrenaline made her stumble a few times. Once he was on the throne, she went to his lap and straddled him. His breath hitched, and she liked how easy it was to affect him.

"Is this what you want?" she asked, her own breathing labored. Her body was pulsing with such a deep need; it scared her how Jasyn could do this to her, but there was a thrill to that fear.

He nodded, not a lick of hesitation.

"What if I'm not who I say I am?"

His hands were on her hips, and they tightened against her, as if making sure a body was actually there and he wasn't dreaming.

"I like whoever you are. I want *you*." He punctuated that last sentence with a soft kiss to her neck.

She closed her eyes, savoring the feel of his lips, but she wouldn't get distracted yet. "Promise to not call me by my name. Call me Sundrop, call me yours, but do *not* use my name."

"Whatever you need, I will give you," Jasyn said breathily.

"Kiss me," she pleaded, and he did.

It was gentle, but his hands on her waist were firm. It was like they were starting where they had left off in the garden. She immediately unbuttoned his shirt, needing to feel his chest, and it urged him to unleash himself. His muscles flexed under her hands, but her mind was entirely on the way his tongue licked, the way his lips sucked. It was alighting her whole body in desire. She rocked her hips against his hardness, and it rubbed at her clit in the perfect way. She was panting already, wanting him deep inside her.

But first, she wanted to give him something to remember her by.

She pulled away, and he was breathing hard, his eyes blown wide. Pushing herself off his lap, she kneeled before him.

"You don't—"

"I want," she simply replied as she undid his pants and rolled them off him.

His erection sprang free, beads of moisture already there for her to suck and swallow.

"Tell me if I'm doing it wrong," she said, and in response, he pushed her dark strands behind her ear.

"I'm learning with you," he said.

She nodded, her nerves high, but she trusted the man in front of her. They would explore this together.

She licked the sides of his shaft in hopes of making it easier for her. Then, she sucked on the head, allowing herself to learn the motions. Jasyn hissed from his seat, his hips bucking upwards. Since he did not stop her, she took it as a sign she was doing something right.

She took a deep breath then sucked as much of his length down as she could. She gagged once he hit the back of her throat, but she relaxed, and it moved deeper. She bobbed her head, his cock moving in and out of her mouth, her eyes filling with tears. She focused on

Jasyn's whimpering sounds. It urged her on; it made her want to pleasure him forever.

A strong moan escaped his lips, and she had no doubt Mych would hear them. Hopefully, he would ensure no one neared the room and heard them too.

"It's my turn," he managed to say between breaths.

She pumped him with her hands; she didn't want to stop, but the pulsing ache between her legs sought release.

"Where do you want me?" she asked.

"Sitting on my face," he replied.

She swallowed, the throbbing heightening at the words. She lifted the dress from her body, and she saw how Jasyn's eyes dilated at the sight of her breasts. They trailed down to the brand, and she shook her head.

"No questions."

He opened his mouth but thankfully followed along. Jasyn shifted to the side and laid down on the throne so his head rested on one armrest and his legs dangled over the other.

"Here." He pointed at his mouth, the demand final.

Iskra didn't question it as she removed her dress and maneuvered herself over top him. He gripped her thighs, making sure she was settled. Without warning, he licked her folds, and she arched her head back in pure ecstasy.

"Gods," she moaned. She was wound so tight, she didn't think she would last long.

He suckled on her clit, and the sensation was so intense, she had to grab the back of the throne to not fall off.

She swayed her hips against his mouth, needing more of him. Through it all, she could hear encouraging words muffled in her pussy.

"My Sundrop."

The words were enough to make her shatter on his tongue, but as soon as she thought she was coming down from her pleasurable high, he inserted a finger inside her. It took her a moment to adjust to the feeling, but as he moved it, a new orgasm brimmed the surface.

"More," she moaned. "More."

He complied by inserting a second finger, and all she could do was grab her breasts and pinch her own nipples. Within moments, a burst of pleasure rocked through her again, and she didn't know if it would ever be enough.

Once she came down, she got off his face. "I want you inside me."

They adjusted themselves so Iskra was sitting on the arm of the throne, the perfect height for Jasyn to line up with her core.

"I'll be slow," he said.

"Don't."

But he didn't seem to listen, because he took his cock in his hands and rubbed it against her clit, around her folds, edging into her entrance before moving away again. He was playing with her, and she liked how it caused her pleasure to rise and fall.

"Ready?" he asked after he toyed with her three times.

She nodded, her eyes shut. She held his shoulders as he entered so slowly, it felt like years before he was fully seated inside her.

"So good, my Sundrop. You feel *so* good." The words came through gritted teeth.

Whimpering at the praise, Iskra pulled him in for a kiss. He started thrusting, and she could cry at the pleasure. He moved at the perfect pace, his hands roaming all over her body. From her nipples to her clit, he never stopped finding ways to remind her he was there, with her, experiencing the same heightened thrill.

When she thought she would fall off the throne arm, he heaved her up. She wrapped her legs around him, and he kept moving inside her as he carried her, the sounds of their slapping flesh echoing around them.

"You're beautiful," he whispered as he feasted on one of her nipples.

He walked her off the dais, into a corner of the throne room covered in plants. It was like they were outside. As her back hit the stone floor, she didn't have a moment to care about the biting cold, because as quickly as he placed her down, he was back inside her. This time, his pace was faster, jagged, uneven. He was close, and seeing him this disheveled was better than flying.

It didn't take long for her to come again, her muscles tightening around his cock, and he soon followed. When she thought he would move on, perhaps lay next to her, he got down to his stomach and sucked on her core again, swallowing the mixture of his own essence and hers to please her again. She was so sensitive, she didn't think her body would let her come, but with the way his tongue pressed down on her clit, she was convulsing within seconds.

After that orgasm, he climbed up her body, kissing her abdomen, her brand, her breasts, until he was at her mouth. She wrapped her arms around his neck.

"I can't wait to marry you," he said earnestly.

Those words were like a burn on her skin, more painful than when she received the brand.

"It'll be a joyous day indeed." She smiled as best as she could, but inside, it was like she was falling with no end in sight.

He nestled his head between her breasts, his fingers skating over her ribs. "Will you tell me where you received such a painful mark?"

Iskra was quiet, remembering the day Kryth discovered her flock of dragons. He trapped her and a few others, and then she was in that shop, and Kryth had that burning metal on her skin. She had yelled in pain, refusing to accept such a fate without letting the Gods hear her cry.

"From someone powerful," Iskra whispered.

"Even more powerful than a future king?"

Iskra didn't have to think twice. "Yes."

Fourteen

They spent the next few hours naked, on top of each other, relishing in the pleasurable bubble they had created. Jasyn couldn't get enough of her taste or her touch. His Sundrop was awakening a feral instinct in him that he had kept locked up his whole life.

He had just devoured her wet cunt again when she jumped to her feet and asked to go outside.

"It's getting late."

Jasyn chuckled as he too got to his feet, legs wobbly from their extensive activities. "The sun is just starting to set."

"And we've been in here since before midday."

He pulled her in, wrapping his arms around her waist. As if on instinct, her arms went around his neck.

"It's not my fault I can't get enough of you," he said into her neck, licking and sucking a pulse point he learned would have her writhing.

Her hand came between them as he continued his ministrations, wrapping around his hardening cock. He hissed as she slid her hand up and down the shaft, tightening around his head, just how he liked it. In response, his hand massaged her breast, squeezing the nipple.

"You're cruel," she said breathily.

"You're majestic." The late sun glowed behind her, and the orangey haze made her look like she was on fire.

"We should take this outside," she repeated, and he knew then he would never be able to deny her anything. He would spend the rest of their lives together serving her. *If* they had that time together, he supposed.

"Anything for you." He knew just the place.

He tugged on her hand, but she yanked backward. She was smiling, and it was so breathtaking, it hurt. "What of our clothes?"

"Mych won't mind."

"Your parents?"

He shrugged, unable to care if they got caught.

"The other guards?" This time, the words came with her crossing her arms under her breast to cover that burned mark.

He wanted to pry further. There was something she was hiding from him, but he figured he had the rest of their marriage to ask her about everything—that was, if he survived the Undertaking. He wanted to know her inside and out, but he promised himself he would fight the hardest to ensure they would have that time. Maybe, even if he lost the Undertaking, she would be willing to follow him, even without a title.

Climbing up to the dais, he grabbed her discarded dress. He bent down, and she stepped into it. As he rolled it up, he pressed kisses to her body, and she shivered under his lips.

He got distracted from dressing her—her mouth was right in front of him, and he was weak, couldn't hold back. Their tongues danced with each other, against the rhythm of their beating hearts.

"Let's go." Her eyes were soft, and he wanted that image stamped in his memory forever.

He got into his pants and led her to the door. He squared his shoulders, and, right as the door opened, Mych stood leisurely in the hall, smirking at them both.

"I hope you both had fun. I had to keep Bron away, and that man is difficult to convince to do anything." Mych shrugged, clearly pleased with himself. "Good thing I like a challenge."

Jasyn rolled his eyes, but his face was on fire, which caused Mych to smile wider.

"We're going to the Butterfly Garden."

"That's quite romantic." Mych winked.

Jasyn bumped his guard's shoulder as he passed him. "No need to keep guard. I don't think you'd want to either."

Esi lightly slapped Jasyn's back. "Heathen."

"I've already heard it all," Mych yelled after them, but Jasyn didn't care. He already had his arm around Esi's shoulders.

Esi gasped at the glass dome in front of her. Like most of the castle, the structure was covered in vines and greenery, with speckles of color coming from flowers.

Jasyn chuckled as he pushed aside the vines and opened the door to allow them both inside.

Esi stilled as she entered. Her mouth was slightly agape, and watching her take in all the sights of the castle had been one of his favorite experiences. This had been his every day since birth, but for her, it was new. The wonder and awe she exuded was contagious. It reminded him of how special the castle was and what an honor it was to live here.

She outstretched her hand, and a butterfly fluttered on her finger. He could have sworn a tear dripped down her cheek.

"I usually hate such small, constricting spaces, but I feel so safe with you," she said. He took in that piece of information and held on to it tightly.

To bring her out of her head, he said. "It used to be just another gazebo where we would all sit and watch the town, but then we begged my parents to turn it into a butterfly sanctuary."

"We?" she asked then flicked his cheek gently. "Or you?"

Even though the structure covered them in shadows, he had no doubt she could see the small stain tinge of color blossoming on his cheeks and ears.

"You know me too well." He grimaced jokingly. "I know so little about you."

Esi snapped her attention to his eyes. "What do you mean?"

"You're keeping secrets—which I don't blame you for, since we've only known each other for a few weeks and are not married yet. But I want to know you."

Esi dipped her head, but he caught her chin with his finger and lifted it. The desire to pry again about that burn mark was strong, but he pushed it back.

"What do you like to do?"

She shook her head. "No one has asked me that before."

Strange, the way she talked about her life. From his point of view, it sounded like she never left her manor, never spoke with anyone. What type of life was that? He would need to speak to her parents and reprimand them for treating their daughter like property kept in a dusty closet.

"So I'm asking you," he said instead, keeping his thoughts to himself.

She shrugged, backing away from his touch, as if embarrassed. "I'm not sure. I like spending time with you. I like your passion for your court, your desire to be a good ruler."

"Although I appreciate the compliments, I want to know about *you*."

She tapped her chin, thinking hard. "I like dancing."

"Why?" he prodded.

It was quiet as she thought again. "Because it's a beautiful feeling to create art with my own body."

In that moment, he wanted nothing more than to call upon an orchestra—perhaps that new up-and-coming one, led by a man named Izyk in the Lightning Court. For now, his hums would have to do.

When the melody came to him, Esi spun around. "What are you—"

But she didn't have a chance to complete the question, because he brought her in close and started swaying to his tune. At first, she was awkward in his arms, but as he guided her, she loosened up. Then, she started leading him. He spun her out and back in his arms, pressing kisses to her lips and cheeks any chance he could.

It was a blissful peace inside the dome, one he never wanted to leave.

"It's getting late," she whispered in the quiet.

"You're always trying to run from me."

"It's for your own good."

As he let her go, she was already on her way out. He followed her, and the sight in front of him had the blood rushing from his face.

Iskra stumbled over her own feet. Esi and Bron were stopped in their tracks, both of their mouths wide open. Iskra's heart stopped at the sight.

"What is going on?"

Jasyn's words were a muffled blur in her ears. She could barely keep herself together, and the thought of turning around and seeing Jasyn's reaction would make her faint.

"Kryth said you were back already," Esi said, but no explanations would get them out of this mess.

Bron patted Esi's lower back. "You should go. Iskra and I can handle this."

He wanted to protect Esi—which Iskra understood—but it didn't hurt any less that Iskra needed to be in the crossfire.

Esi made one step, but Jasyn shook his head. "She stays. You all tell me what's happening, what the minister has to do with all this."

Iskra finally faced the man she had fallen in love with, and the coldness on his face seized something in her chest.

"Jasyn..." Iskra said.

"Tell. Me."

The anger in his tone had her stepping back a bit as she composed herself. Esi seemed to want to take charge as she stepped to Iskra's side. Bron muttered under his breath for Esi to stay put, but clearly, she wasn't going to listen to him.

Jasyn's eyes bounced between the two of them, and the last few weeks must have flashed before his eyes.

Esi cleared her throat. "When I arrived, I stumbled upon Iskra and Kryth, though he didn't appear as the minister to us then. I saw an opportunity for one last sliver of freedom before our marriage. I asked her to take my place—"

"During the day," Jasyn completed the statement for her.

Esi nodded. "While I was out with Dominik."

Iskra didn't think Jasyn could look sicker, but that sentence alone proved her wrong.

"Then who are you?" Jasyn asked Iskra directly, his green eyes gazing deeply into her soul, seeking answers she wouldn't give.

"No one. I'm a fraud."

She peered behind her, where the sun would be gone for the night soon. She needed to go. Jasyn followed her line of sight, and his eyes narrowed.

"I'm sorry," she whispered, taking him in. This, without a doubt, would be the last time she saw him before he had a blade to her chest to kill her. He didn't need to know that, though.

"Take care of him," were Iskra's parting words to Esi before she ran off through the copse of plants, tears burning her eyes.

Fifteen

"I understand if you want to end the betrothal," Esi—the *real* Esi—said. She didn't seem bothered or worried that the truth was now out in the open. Perhaps it was because her guard was right behind her, ready to snatch her away if Jasyn threatened her. It would be fruitless. Jasyn was the one in power here.

Wiping the frustration from his eyes, Jasyn leaned against a nearby tree, desperate for something sturdy to hold him up. His body was still on fire from the last few hours. What he and...Iskra had done together was stamped all over his skin.

Esi must have noticed his panic, because she came up to him. "Based on the fact you're not wearing a shirt, I think Iskra followed through on what she wanted. What I granted permission for her to do."

Jasyn snapped his head to her. "But I just fucked someone who was lying about their identity. I thought I was sleeping with my future wife, not some...some commoner." The word burned his tongue. He hated thinking about Iskra like that, even in anger.

"Yet, you felt it was right. You felt a connection with her and acted on your desire to meld your souls in the most beautiful way." Esi's words were filled with so much air, like she was floating amongst the clouds and wanted him to join her.

"Are you saying I should marry her instead of you?"

"I'm saying I would rather us find ways to be happy in our marriage, even if it's outside each other."

Jasyn scoffed breathily. "So you and Dominik can continue your daily rendezvous?"

The way Bron stiffened was palpable. He didn't like this Dominik one bit, and if he read it correctly, Esi's guard wished it was he who had the lady's affection.

"Those rendezvous will become less frequent once you win the Undertaking, save our court for one more year, and become crowned. But yes, so I can still have Dominik in my life."

"And I'll have Iskra?"

The silence that followed was loud. Bron had his head dipped to the ground while Esi's eyes spoke of sadness. What was he missing?

Before he had an opportunity to prod, he heard the squeaking of a wheel.

His parents appeared before them, giddy and so much at ease. His mother was on his father's lap as he rolled them down the paths.

"Oh." His mother placed a hand over her heart, as if they had startled her. "I wasn't expecting you here."

His father eyed his son's exposed chest. "Hopefully, you're behaving."

Esi and Bron had their eyes on Jasyn. It was a test, he supposed. Would he reveal it all now? It would end the betrothal. He thought then about that little girl from this morning who had approached Esi—or who they all thought was Esi—with that flower crown. She had adored the lady in front of her. Jasyn couldn't rip away the image the two of them created.

"I was just showing them the Butterfly Garden." Jasyn gestured. Then, he narrowed his eyes. What were his parents doing? They never came out here. At least, he thought they never did, but he saw the blankets and basket his mother was holding, and thoughts of what that meant swirled in his head. "We should go."

Jasyn started walking away, pushing Bron and Esi along with him. He glanced behind him before the Butterfly Garden was out of sight, and he saw the way his parents giggled as they entered. Before the door shut, he saw the flutter of butterflies swarm them. His parents had been lucky to find love in their marriage. He wished that could be him too, but he decided then, he would marry Esi if he won the Undertaking. After all, his responsibility was to the people of the Sun Court, and he would do everything he could to prove himself worthy.

Iskra's knees buckled in the town streets. She didn't have time to wallow in her own pity. The sun would set soon, and she didn't need to cause a disastrous scene in front of children.

She couldn't believe this was how it ended. She thought she had a few more blissful days with him. She wanted to be in his arms, to soak up his scent and his touch.

"I knew you would come crawling back to me," Kryth's voice whispered.

She wiped the snot from her nose. She had been so distracted by her own woes, she hadn't heard him approaching.

He crouched so he was eye level with her, his minister blue eyes piercing. "Sometimes, it's best to stay in a cage. It's safer there."

Right now, she only found truth in that statement, because the pain coursing through her was immense, like she was being burned from the inside.

Her life prior to Kryth had been so short, she barely remembered it. She knew she had lived in a commune of dragon shifters. She knew they were constantly on edge because of the possibility of being caught. In the back of her memories, she knew she felt at peace there with the other dragon shifters. They had more control of their shifting, and she could transform any time of day.

Then, Kryth took her away. He had killed his sister and put his nephew, Bron, in debt, knowing he was never going to heal her. He was a villain who ripped joy from others' lives so he could maintain a title he didn't deserve.

Yet, even if she despised him, he was all she knew. His shop had become her home, and she had nowhere else to run.

"Take me to the shop," she whispered, unable to deal with her emotions anymore.

So, Kryth helped her up and carried his prized possession to her cage.

Sixteen

There weren't enough windows to distract Iskra from her sorrows. She had resorted to washing the neighboring shops' windows just to keep her mind on the present instead of the painful past and the tragic future in front of her. Even if her pruned hands told her she had done enough, she could still find another window to clean somewhere.

She must have looked like a rabid animal, because townspeople sidestepped her and avoided her gaze. It was funny how just days before, she was with Jasyn, passing out desserts to them, yet now, they didn't recognize her at all. Though that wasn't a fair assessment. Her hair was back to its auburn color, and she had been hiding her face by wearing a bonnet. It was to protect against the sun, she told herself. In reality, she feared someone *would* notice the similarities between the window washer and the prince's betrothed. She didn't want to cause any more trouble for Jasyn and his family. It was better to protect them from damaging rumblings in any way she could.

She heaved the bucket with dirty water and threw it out into the grassy field. Rubbing her aching back, Iskra headed back to the shop.

It had been her routine the last few days: leave her cage, get water from the river, start cleaning, and return to the shop right before nightfall.

Just like clockwork, Kryth was outside the shop with his pipe in hand. She swatted away the smoke as she entered the shop, but Kryth grabbed her wrist.

"Your princeling is in Ogrod, visiting Lady Esi's family," he gloated. "He's asking for her hand in marriage."

"That seems like a wasteful trip. Her parents and the royal family have already decided their fates." She hated the sting in her words. She was jealous of a reality that existed long before she ever met Jasyn.

Kryth noted her tone, though, because he smiled with malicious glee. "It's a shame you won't be here to witness the wedding. I'm sure the streets will be partying for days to celebrate."

"Are you that confident he'll kill me and get the Heart?"

Kryth took a puff of his pipe, and Iskra coughed as the smoke hit her nose.

"I never said the wedding between the current prince and her. Perhaps my nephew wins like he clearly needs. Either way, whoever is the victor will be marrying the lady."

"If the victor is a she?"

"I have no doubts Lady Esi's family could care less who is on that throne. They just want her as consort."

Iskra wanted to rip Kryth's throat, but she didn't have the strength. "How could you force your own nephew to resort to gambling in order to pay you back for failing to keep your sister alive?"

Kryth didn't seem shocked by the question. In fact, he avoided it at first, fully stepping back inside the shop. He tinkered with the glass bottles, making sure they were perfectly set on the shelves.

"She wanted to take this away from me."

"The shop?"

Kryth nodded. "She hated the idea of me becoming minister. She said it would corrupt my mind, like it corrupted all ministers before me."

"She had a point," Iskra muttered under her breath, and Kryth didn't seem impressed by her as he snapped his attention away from the opaque glass bottles.

"My sister didn't understand the importance of my role, and the Gods cursed her for it," Kryth explained. "Why would I have interfered with their judgement?"

Iskra shivered at his words. There was no remorse in the way he spoke. Kryth truly believed his sister—Bron's mother—deserved her death.

"Have the Gods even shown you who wins?"

"My job as minister is to ensure I get a dragon in that cave with the Heart."

"What good is having those Sight powers then?"

"They're a guide. They beckon me to pick the right dragon for that year. Like you." He pointed the pipe at her. "I felt compelled to pick you this year. Perhaps it was to give Jasyn someone to fuck before he dies like his siblings." Iskra growled, and Kryth smirked. "I see those creaturely urges want to come out."

"Don't provoke me."

Clearly, he would be doing the exact opposite. "Too bad you won't be able to say your goodbyes. He returns from his travels the night before the Undertaking. I'll already be transferring you to the cave by then."

Iskra closed her eyes. Every day, she wanted to apologize to him, to run to the castle, get on her knees, and explain it all. It was better he didn't know the full truth, though.

"Will you pass a letter to him if he comes out alive?" she asked.

He grabbed her chin. "For you, my Iskra, I will."

Jasyn had his hands folded in his lap, looking out the carriage window. The last few days had been a performance. He had to act like he was joyful at the prospect of marrying Lady Esi in front of her family. He had to act like he wasn't terrified of the Undertaking tomorrow. Hardest of all, he had to act like his heart hadn't been ripped out and that he didn't miss Iskra. It was foolish to even allow his mind to wander to her. His future wife was in front of him. He would marry her and be loyal to her while Esi could do whatever she pleased. It was a promise he'd made to himself. A sacrifice owed in honor of his dead siblings.

"Can this move any faster?" Esi hit the roof of the carriage, as if that would quicken the pace.

"What is the rush?" he snapped, and he hated that he sounded so harsh. He was angry she was the one who came up with the plan to have Iskra switch places with her, but he didn't blame her. It wasn't like she had much of a choice in their engagement. It was the reason he took this trip with her, to show his dedication and give her one last chance to back out. Right before they left her parents' home, he went down on one knee and proposed. She said yes, but even then, he knew her heart was set on another.

Was that why she was in a rush? Perhaps Esi and Dominik had a midnight rendezvous planned.

"If we go any faster, we'll crash into the trees," Bron grumbled.

"I'll save you if we do." Mych smiled in response.

Bron side-eyed Mych and shook his head in exasperation. Mych didn't seem deterred.

"Cheer up." Mych tapped Bron's foot with his own. "Once the Undertaking is over, we'll officially be working together. Isn't that an exciting prospect?"

Jasyn chuckled, if only to add some warmth to the chilly carriage.

"Are you confident your prince will even win?"

Mych crossed his arms, and for some reason, Jasyn anxiously anticipated his answer. It was rare for someone to openly talk about the possibility of Jasyn losing—or worse, dying. Too many people tried to push optimism. Jasyn needed reality.

"Jasyn is beyond equipped to win tomorrow."

Bron stared down Jasyn intensely, and it caused a pit in his stomach. Something was off about him.

"We'll see once tomorrow comes and Jasyn is faced with the dangers and twists of the Undertaking." Bron smiled at him.

"We're close!" Esi exclaimed as she clapped her hands.

Jasyn snuck a peek outside the window, where it was still daylight. They left a few hours earlier at Esi's request.

They weren't at the castle, though, and Esi was calling for the carriage to stop.

"What is happening?" Mych asked.

Jasyn would like to know too, but Esi was practically jumping outside the carriage and yanking on Jasyn's arm to follow her.

He stumbled out, and he had to blink to adjust to the light.

"Where are we?"

"Hurry," Esi only called back to him. He could hear Mych and Bron's footsteps behind them, and Jasyn was very aware how he must look to the townspeople: frantic and confused. Not the image he was trying to exude, but he had to follow his future wife through the streets.

He caught up to Esi right as they turned a corner, and Jasyn's heart stilled at the sight.

Iskra was there, sitting on the ground as she leaned against a shop wall. Her knees were folded in so she had a place to set a parchment, and from this angle, he could clearly see her handwriting. She was focused, her eyes narrowed in on whatever words she needed to let out. It was painful to see her again. Her hair no longer matched Esi's inky locks, instead a deep shade of brown-red. In the sunlight, it almost looked like a dark flame.

Having both Esi and Iskra there made him wonder how he ever thought they were the same person. Yes, when they had the same hair, their features were similar, but looking at Iskra was like being in a meadow of flowers. It was overwhelming. Every inch was beautiful, and it was hard to focus on one thing. Iskra's nose sloped a bit higher than Esi's. Her freckles were more pronounced. The way she viewed the world was like seeing it for the first time. She clearly wasn't a well-traveled or experienced woman like Lady Esi. Yet, the compulsion to get on his knees was still there. He wanted to crawl to her, to cradle her in his arms. He had to fist his hands to stop himself.

"Why are we here?"

His words snapped Iskra's attention to him, and her face blanched.

Esi pushed him forward slightly. "You owe yourself—owe each other—a goodbye. I have no doubts your promise to remain loyal to me is true, but it doesn't mean you shouldn't have the chance to at least close this door so you can live in our marriage with a settled heart."

Jasyn bit his tongue, wanting to yell that he didn't need this right now, but Iskra had gotten up, and she was just staring and staring at him. He could read the regret on her face, could see the shaking of her hands gripping that parchment.

"Go," Esi whispered.

Slone spare him, he did.

Iskra didn't move from her spot. She was letting him control the scene. It only took him a few strides to be right in front of her, so close, she had to crane her neck slightly just to look at him.

He wanted to wrap his hand around the back of her neck, bring her close, kiss her until he was dizzy with the fill of her, until he forgot everything except for the way she made him feel.

He kept the small distance between them instead.

"I'm sorry." Her voice was weary, nervous.

He licked his teeth, hating that the words affected him. He should be unruffled. After all, this woman lied to him. Everything between them was a lie, and the time they shared meant nothing. She was playing a part.

"I understand if you want nothing from me, if you don't want to hear a word from my mouth ever again." She extended the paper towards him. "I wrote this. You can read or burn it. It's your choice."

He stared at the paper too long. Taking it was a choice. Ignoring it was one too. The paper was in his hands before he could even register he had taken it from her.

"You're a good person, Jasyn. You'll make a great king, one who is not blinded by desire. Let your light shine so you can win this." She leaned forward with her arm out, slowly, giving him a moment to pull back. He didn't. Her hand was on his chest, right over his heart.

"You have taken my heart. Let it come alive. It is now only here to serve you."

Jasyn narrowed his eyes. It sounded like she was swearing fealty, and it made him squirm. It wasn't right. In the deepest pits of his heart, she was the woman in his bed each night.

"Thank you for everything, Iskra."

They were the only words he could offer, but they conveyed exactly what he needed. She had changed him in such a short time, given him the confidence and courage to believe if he won the crown, he could be a good ruler. If he did win the Undertaking, he would be sure to come back here and thank her again.

"Iskra!" a voice yelled from inside one of the shops.

Iskra flinched, and it made him want to investigate the source of the noise. Who had caused Iskra such fear that she couldn't take the sound of their voice?

As if she read his thoughts, she shook her head.

"I must go." She curtsied in the slightly wobbly way she always did, another obvious differentiator between the two women. He would miss seeing it. "Good luck tomorrow, Prince Jasyn."

He was left alone with nothing but a parchment and his soul ripped from his chest.

Seventeen

Jasyn ignored the letter. He told himself he would only read it if he came out of the Undertaking alive. There was no point in considering Iskra's words if he would be dead by tonight.

He spent the night before trying to sleep, and when that didn't work, he went outside and gardened. Mych joined him, disapproving of his nightly activity.

"You'll be tired," he had said.

"I'll be calm," Jasyn had responded.

So, they worked together in silence for a few hours before he finally let himself sleep until the morning sun rose.

Now, he trekked behind Mych, who led him to the cave where the Undertaking would transpire. As he walked the streets, townspeople bowed their heads, children running up to him to give him pebbles or flowers or baked goods. He placed his hand on his chest in thanks for each one.

When he passed a specific road, he eyed a shop he had never entered. He knew that inside was one of the most important things in his life. It was a scary revelation how much Iskra meant to him.

It was even scarier to realize their paths would never converge in the same way as before.

It wasn't much longer before they were at the opening of the cave, the wide expanse looking like a mouth that would swallow him and the other competitors whole.

Last year, he was here saying his goodbyes to his sister and father, where, hours later, he only greeted his father again. Another competitor had been carrying him on his back, the one who had ensured his father continued his rulership. That competitor was now living comfortably, no longer worrying about his pockets ever emptying.

Today, it was just his parents there.

His mother crashed into him. "My boy."

There were tears in her eyes, and he did everything he could to only instill confidence in his mother. He didn't cry or show any sign of fear.

His father patted his arm, and Jasyn bent to give him a hug too. This was the first time in thirty-one years he wasn't entering the dragon's den. He couldn't imagine the swirl of emotions.

"Come back to us," his father whispered. "I don't care about the titles anymore. Just come back."

Jasyn hitched a breath. His whole life, his father had drilled into him and his siblings the importance of keeping the crown within the family, but after losing two of his children, his father's priorities must have changed.

"I'll do my best," he told his father.

He could hear his mother's sniffles as he left. Right before entering the cave, he caught a quick glimpse of the minister. Kryth seemed calm, and it was eerie to think about how the minister was connected to the gods. Did he already know who would be leaving this alive? Jasyn tried not to stare too closely, but the minister noticed his gaze because he gave Jasyn a bright smile, like he was satisfied already with the outcome.

Iskra had been given a few more hours of freedom the night before the Undertaking, a gift from Kryth. She spent it by the river, picking grass and weaving it together. She wondered what Jasyn was doing. It was a beautiful night, the stars above them twinkling. Since she had been trapped by Kryth, she hadn't seen the night sky, save for the night of the party. She soaked it in now, the beauty of the darkness surrounding her.

Children ran by her, parents scolding them for getting their clothes dirty, but Iskra was not bothered once. Until Kryth came to retrieve her at first dawn, she hadn't realized how long she had been outside.

They walked to the cave, and she felt so overcome with emotions: regret, longing, fear, sadness. Before diving into the dark, she took one last look at the bright world around her and took a deep breath. Then, she entered with her head high.

Jasyn would win this, become king, and live a full, happy life, she promised herself.

The tunnel to enter the cave was tight, but then, a large cavern expanded in front of him. It was daunting, knowing that in a few minutes, the room—lit by skylights above—would be covered in blood. Would his own body be ripped to shreds?

"Prince Jasyn." The familiar voice made Jasyn still, along with Mych, who was next to him.

"Bron?" Mych's voice was small, hurt.

Bron smiled at them both, answering a question Jasyn had before he could even ask. "Who wouldn't take the chance to be king? All that money was too hard to pass up."

"Does Lady Esi know?" Jasyn asked, confused. There were signs Bron had been interested in his lady, but Jasyn would never expect him to go this far, especially when Esi had her heart set on Dominik.

"She'll know once I'm the victor."

"And Dominik?" Mych's arms were crossed, a defense against the pain. Jasyn didn't know what—if anything—transpired between them, but clearly, there was enough weight there now that it affected Mych.

Bron's eyes hardened. "She can do whatever she pleases with him. I'm not here because of her."

"Why not seek a different future for yourself? Is power more important than a true connection with someone?" Mych's voice was cold.

If Jasyn saw it correctly, Bron's face softened. "I'm sorry." The guard's voice cracked, revealing the sincerity of those simple words. "I know we discussed a future in which we would be working side-by-side, but I don't know if being Esi and Jasyn's guard would be enough to fulfill what I need."

Jasyn squinted at Bron. There was more to this story.

"Then you have no imagination if you think our only options are being guards or you becoming king." Mych turned to Jasyn. "Good luck, Your Highness."

Jasyn bowed his head. "Thank you for all your work."

They hugged each other quickly, and Mych left without sparing Bron a glance.

"He's right." Jasyn said.

Bron whipped his head in his direction.

"You two would have had my blessing to leave your work and live your lives away from the castle if you desired it. Hopefully, that future is still possible—if we make it out alive."

Bron shook his head, and Jasyn saw a deep sadness cross his face, like he didn't truly want this either, but he had been cornered into it.

Jasyn didn't have a chance to pry for answers, because a large bell sounded, and the competitors focused on the minister. Kryth seemed ravenous for a good show as he smiled at them, his hands occupied with a bundle of smoking, burning herbs. The stench was strong, and Jasyn wondered what exactly the point was.

"The Undertaking will begin shortly. There is only one rule: fight until one of you gets the Heart, or the court will burn to ash."

Jasyn swallowed, thinking about Iskra. A part of him wished he had read the letter, but it would have only distracted him.

"Please position yourselves," the minister announced. "When I ring this bell again, my fierce dragon will come out and begin this all."

Eighteen

The bell echoed in the cavern, but he barely heard it as the dragon flew overhead, its large form a looming shadow, showcasing the monstrosity they were about to face. Kryth stormed away, no doubt running somewhere he would be safe with a view of the cavern.

Jasyn took a stance as he pulled the sword from his sheath, but his legs were heavy, like roots had clawed their way around his ankles and held him down. None of the competitors wore armor, as it would be too constricting for climbing. The dragon perched itself on a ledge, its reddish-brown scales gleaming in the sun from the spotlight above it. Its amber eyes practically shone as the beast assessed the space.

Jasyn didn't have time to admire it, because before he could blink, the dragon dove from its spot.

The competitors scattered, and Jasyn ran behind a boulder to cover himself, sheathing his sword. Heat scorched the area, and he knew the dragon would not take it easy on them. Jasyn thought back to his siblings, how scared they must have been, of his father, who had been thrown across this very cavern. He wondered how many people would die today.

Someone shouted, the sound loud in his ears. But it was the way it quickly became silent again that had Jasyn gripping the hilt of his sword tighter.

He couldn't hide for long, but he took the advantageous position he was in to let his eyes scour. There were numerous ledges climbing high up the walls. The Heart could be on one of those. He'd need to find a way to get up to each of them, or at least one at the highest point to be able to look down. There were some ropes he could use to hoist himself up, but he reconsidered that option. After all, rope burned.

Jasyn crawled away from the boulder and saw the dragon was on the same ledge again, waiting. Unlike the participants, the dragon seemed to be in no rush. It would gladly drag this out, causing the tension to build.

Jasyn wondered if the Heart was right on that ledge, the dragon protecting the precious ruby. There was no guarantee, and Jasyn would rather search lower before committing to the high climb, but...

As if hearing Jasyn's doubts, the dragon practically snapped its attention to Jasyn. With widened eyes, Jasyn took a step back, uncomfortable with the scrutiny.

"Watch it, prince." One of the competitors shoved him, running toward one of the walls. She was lithe, easily hauling herself upwards using the small pockets within the rock. Jasyn watched in awe at the technique.

Others took her lead, following on other sides of the cavern, like they trusted she knew something.

Jasyn had his eyes on the dragon again. It seemed to be focused on itself now, so this would be the time to attempt something. Instead of going up, Jasyn decided to go down into the crater. If the dragon attacked, there at least wouldn't be a big fall below him.

The terrain was steep, and he almost tumbled too many times, but he wouldn't stop. He had one goal in mind: the Heart, the Heart, the Heart. He repeated it in his head like it was his own heartbeat, pumping the adrenaline through his veins.

A yell reached his ear, and he had to watch the woman who had been stealthy and quick fall. It seemed so fast, but he had no doubt the journey down must have felt like hours. The crunch of bones crackled in his ears. The cohort of ten original competitors were now down to eight.

The crater in the cavern kept going down, hiding spots peppering its walls. He brought out some of his light into his hands, allowing him to get a better look.

There was a tight alcove in one section, and Jasyn crawled inside to inspect its depths. It didn't lead far, and there was no Heart to be found. Jasyn took a moment to sulk in disappointment. Of course it wouldn't be that easy. With it being such a tight fit, Jasyn had to move backwards, exposing himself in ways he didn't like. He nudged himself out quickly.

Still hidden from view, Jasyn looked up again to see the dragon beginning its vicious attacks on the competitors. One of them was on a ledge, sword in one hand and flames in the other. He swiped the sword as the dragon got closer to him, but the action only resulted in him stepping too far off the ledge. He slipped, and Jasyn winced as the man fell off, barely able to grasp the rock to stop him from falling. The competitor hung there, but with one hand occupied with the sword, he wouldn't be able to swing himself back to safety.

Even from a distance, Jasyn could see the competitor contemplating his next move. He let go of the sword, but it was fruitless, because the dragon flew by, causing the competitor to lose his grip. Jasyn closed his eyes this time, unable to stomach the sight of another death. He took that as his cue to move. This wouldn't end until someone killed the dragon and got the Heart.

"You," said a voice Jasyn dreaded hearing.

Jasyn put up the one hand not holding a sword in surrender. "Bron."

Bron looked feral, and Jasyn saw his sleeve had been burnt, revealing welted red skin beneath. Jasyn wondered if that was from the dragon or another competitor.

"There's only one outcome here," Bron warned.

"Esi will never forgive you if I end up dead." Those were not the right words. Jasyn could now trust that Bron's decision to enter the Undertaking was beyond Esi.

Bron snorted. "What gives you the right to say that? You barely know her. You've spent every waking minute with that fraud, Iskra."

A low growl reverberated from the back of Jasyn's throat, and he had no idea why he was defensive of a woman who had lied to him.

"What about Mych?"

"That was one night." But the words sounded shallow from Bron's lips, like he couldn't even convince himself of the lie.

"It could be more."

Jasyn knew, with the way Bron was stalking towards him, that no words would convince him to stop this madness. Bron was on a mission, and Jasyn needed to learn what exactly was pushing him. Jasyn tightened his grip on the hilt of his sword as Bron neared. He stuck his blade out so Bron wouldn't get too close.

"It doesn't have to end this way," Jasyn pleaded. "There is a reality in which we both come out alive."

Bron circled him, and Jasyn had to turn to keep eyes on him. Bron's sword was still, hand on the hilt, like he was assessing before he committed to the inevitable squabble.

"But there is only one outcome in which I end up king. And you need to be dead for the people to accept me as their new ruler."

Finally, Bron unsheathed his blade, and Jasyn backed up to create distance between them. Bron smirked, but Jasyn didn't care if he appeared cowardly for choosing to be strategic. He wanted to save his energy.

"Put down the sword," Jasyn said, more harsh now. "Let's both search for the Heart instead of acting on this petty fight you've concocted in your head."

Those words hit some mark in Bron, because his sword came slashing toward Jasyn in quick, effortless moves, forcing Jasyn to back away further. Jasyn was on defense, but he expected nothing less when fighting a trained guard.

Jasyn blocked the attack, but Bron wasn't discouraged. He was smiling widely, hungry for this fight, while Jasyn could barely take a deep breath. He had trained for years for the Undertaking, but it didn't equip him for something so personal. Being a prince should have clued him in on that possibility, but for most of his life, the idea of entering was never on the horizon. It was always meant to be Jaymes, and when he died, Dahlia was to rule.

Jasyn heard a scream in the distance, and he winced at another death. He regretted being so distracted, because Bron started attacking in earnest, his movements nonstop and fast. Jasyn parried the oncoming thrust in his direction, and he managed to get a hit on Bron's arm.

Bron grunted in pain as the slice hit the burn marks, and Jasyn used the moment to his advantage, re-centering himself. A shadow eclipsed them, but Jasyn refused to look up to see where the dragon headed. He just hoped it wasn't towards them.

"You don't deserve the crown," Bron spat. "Prince Jaymes and Princess Dahlia should be here."

Unlike Bron, Jasyn understood the tactic, and he wouldn't let the words hit their intended mark. Esi—or, he should say, Iskra—showed him how he could lead, how he was good at it if he built up his confidence. He did deserve the crown, as long as he continued to rule with kindness. With Iskra's help, he could survive the throne and thrive on it.

"I can't turn back time," Jasyn said. "They're gone, and now, I must push forward."

Bron slashed again, his movements growing hurried. He wasn't liking how the conversation was going, it seemed. It was making his moves frantic, and Jasyn had no choice but to keep his distance.

Jasyn hissed as Bron cut near his shoulder, the pain slicing across his whole body. He didn't allow himself to look at the damage, because Bron kept advancing.

Without the onslaught, Jasyn had no time to analyze his next move. His only goal was to ensure neither of them got hurt.

In his desperation, Jasyn didn't notice the hole in the ground. His ankle twisted, and he fell backwards. His body screamed at him as he hit the ground. He lost his grip on his sword, and Bron was on top of him in seconds.

Bron leaned down so he could whisper in Jasyn's ear. "Perhaps these words will affect you then: I hope you are able to sleep at night after killing Iskra."

At first, everything was a blur. Jasyn's eyes moved wildly, trying to comprehend his statement, but it didn't make sense until Bron clarified. His words pierced his heart more intensely than a sword ever could.

"Iskra is a dragon shifter, and you'll need to kill her to get the Heart."

Nineteen

"No." Jasyn shook his head frantically, his breathing hurried and unstable. Bron was lying, trying to throw Jasyn off guard. Iskra was safe at that shop.

Flames licked at Jasyn's neck, and he screamed in pain, the sound guttural. He didn't realize he had the capacity to yell like that. Jasyn didn't have a moment to recover, though, because Bron held the tip of the sword right under Jasyn's chin. If he moved too quickly, the blade would pierce his skin.

"Maybe it's a good thing I plan to win this and end her instead," Bron announced like it was nothing, like he didn't plan to end a precious life.

"No," Jasyn said, more forcefully this time. "You aren't touching her."

Right on cue, the dragon—*Iskra*—flew over them, and his heart broke. His mind couldn't wrap around the fact that the dragons were shifters, people all along.

"She's not herself anymore. She's just a wild beast, thanks to Kryth."

"Don't you dare speak of her like that," Jasyn growled. Even if she had lied to him, his mind couldn't let her go. He couldn't imagine his life without her. His Sundrop had been the best part of his life after years of grief and pain, and he wouldn't let some traitor near her.

His anger and defensiveness manifested as a burst of energy. He spit in Bron's face and used the quick moment of distraction. Jasyn fumbled as he grabbed his fallen sword and rammed the end of the hilt in Bron's temple. He didn't want to kill him. There was still a deeper truth lingering in the air, and he had the desire to learn it.

As Bron yelled in pain, Jasyn moved into a fighting stance. His whole body hurt, and the burn stung as he moved his neck, but he didn't care about that.

He approached Bron until they were practically chest to chest.

"You will not kill her." Jasyn enunciated each word, making sure Bron absorbed each syllable.

"If it's not me, it's you or another competitor. She must die so someone can get the Heart."

There was another way. There had to be. Iskra's life couldn't end, not when he felt like he had so much to say to her. He didn't know what the future would look like. He would be marrying Lady Esi, but the future had to at least have Iskra alive.

Jasyn looked up to find Iskra perched again on the highest ledge. Her body was relaxed, as if she was bored, waiting for whoever attempted to climb up next. He didn't know where the rest of the competitors were, or if any more were alive aside from Jasyn and Bron.

We're both coming out of this alive, Jasyn thought to himself as he took her in. He only got to see the real Iskra for a short time, but it was hard to forget the auburn shade of her hair and how it perfectly matched the scales of her dragon or those amber eyes. He had been falling for those eyes, dreaming about them. They were like precious jewels, more valuable than any crown.

His next steps were unplanned, but he needed to act fast.

"You'll only be killed if you think you can get the Heart without ending her first."

Jasyn ignored Bron's words, even if they poked at exactly where his mind was headed.

"I'd be more worried about what your life will look like if you come out of this alive, Bron," Jasyn spoke clearly, without any fear of what was to come. "You betrayed the trust of so many. Was it worth it?"

Bron smiled, but it wasn't a sign of glee or pleasure. It was like he was laughing at the dire situation, recognizing the ridiculousness of it. He didn't want to be here, Jasyn took a guess.

As Jasyn left Bron, he ran out of the crater, never taking his eyes off Iskra. She was his priority now.

Iskra, Iskra, Iskra, Jasyn repeated in his mind until he convinced himself the dragon above was actually her. He wasn't fighting a beast—he was fighting for his love.

His foot slipped on a loose rock as the realization dawned on him.

He loved Iskra. Every day over the last few weeks, he had spent almost every waking moment with her. Not Esi. He barely knew Esi at all. No, if he survived this, if he left with the Heart in his hand, he would be marrying a stranger. Esi was a lady, a woman of noble blood a prince like him would be expected to marry as he took the throne, not a commoner like Iskra.

That truth might have been scarier than the impending confrontation with Iskra in her dragon form.

He wondered then how she arrived in this mess. He knew the bare details of how the minister picked a dragon from his collection each year, but he never questioned *how* he got them, never realized they were people who shifted. His parents had frowned upon asking too many questions because it would make the royal family appear as if they didn't trust the minister or the Weather Gods themselves.

Jasyn had no plan as he reached one of the cave's walls. He put his sword back in its sheath and prayed Slone would have mercy on him.

"I'm coming," Jasyn whispered to himself as he found holes in the walls to propel his body upward.

He knew Iskra was still perched because it was quiet. He hoped there was no other infighting between the competitors. There was no point in killing each other, not when they could come out of this alive, *together*, if Jasyn got the Heart. Deep in his soul, Jasyn hoped it also meant Iskra would come out of this alive too.

He had an idea in mind, but his mind swirled with doubts about his abilities. Then, he remembered the confidence Iskra had taught him to hold.

Jasyn grit his teeth as he scaled up the wall, his legs and arms shaking with the exertion. No matter how hard his body wanted to betray him, he wouldn't allow himself to fall. He just had to make it up to the first ledge, and then, he could rest.

With each strenuous heave upward, Jasyn continued to repeat Iskra's name. It was all for her, he decided just then. Even if he had to die to ensure she lived through this, he would.

A blaze of heat hit his back, along with a gust of wind. Iskra was on the move, and he needed to act fast before she caused him to stumble.

He didn't take his attention away from his current goal. He secured his left hand in a small pocket, anchored his right foot on a small bulge in the wall, and pushed himself up again. He didn't stop his momentum. He only had to make it a bit farther, and he would be safe—at least as safe as one could be in this situation.

When he swung his leg up on the ledge, he hugged the ground beneath him and stayed there longer than he should. Rolling onto his back, he finally caught a glimpse of his surroundings again.

Iskra was on the same ledge, still much higher than him. It would take a long time to get to her spot.

Then, movement on the opposite side of the cave caught his attention. He turned his head and saw a competitor climbing up one of the ropes. She was ahead of Jasyn, but she was being reckless with her speed. She'd tire quickly, and that would put her in danger of slipping up.

He saw large shadows move, and he knew Iskra was growing antsy. She wanted another fight, so Jasyn did the dumbest thing he could think of: he yelled.

"Get on the next ledge and stay there!" With the way the competitor was rushing, it looked like she planned to bypass the next ledge to keep going without a break.

Jasyn was now standing, his body tense as he watched the competitor near the ledge. He was about to take a breath of relief, as she seemed to get there before Iskra flew down at her. Just as he relaxed, the competitor skipped over the ledge to keep climbing.

"Fuck," he swore to himself.

No amount of training could have prepared him for this, Jasyn realized. The Undertaking was worse than a nightmare. How did his father compete countless times and win? How did he watch so many people die and come out so unfazed, or at least act like it? This would shake Jasyn's worldview for life.

"Watch out!" Jasyn called out, naively hopeful the competitor would heed his warning and turn back to the ledge.

Instead, Iskra was flying straight towards the competitor, breathing fire. Jasyn watched the rope burn. He winced as he heard a scream, but Jasyn didn't have a chance to check what happened to the competitor because Iskra was now heading straight for him.

Jasyn quickly pulled his sword out, but just as she neared him, she shot upward again. He expected her to rest on her perch, but she skipped past that. She dove, flew directly at him, and tilted up right before she slammed into him. She looped around again and again.

She was taunting him, he realized. He couldn't make any progress to the next ledge if she kept at this.

He had to find another way up.

"Jasyn, you bastard!" Bron called from somewhere too close for Jasyn's liking.

When Iskra was flying, Jasyn peeked over the side of the ledge and saw Bron on his way.

"You're being impulsive," Jasyn warned him.

With one last stretch, Bron was on the ledge with Jasyn. Bron's sword was in his sheath, but Jasyn guessed that would be temporary. Jasyn had to keep moving.

Iskra was now shooting for them, and Bron crouched to cover himself. Jasyn only had his attention on Iskra and found there was no familiarity or warmth in her eyes.

"She's not herself anymore," Bron said, evidently noticing Jasyn's devastation. "I'll kill her, and this will end a lot easier."

Jasyn closed his eyes and shook his head.

"You're letting emotion get in the way of this," Bron continued.

Jasyn flinched as he felt Iskra fly by them and back up again, completing the same circle.

"And *your* emotions are not clouding *your* actions?" Jasyn snapped, ready to finally get answers.

"You have no idea what brought me here." Bron's voice was deep and guttural. "You get to hide in that glass castle of yours, but others, like me, live in a world where we have to sacrifice and yet leave empty-handed."

Jasyn was trying to follow Bron's words, but the guard was being vague. It frustrated Jasyn that he wouldn't spit it out.

"Why are you here? Tell me, and I might even be able to help."

Bron scoffed, and his reaction only angered Jasyn more. "You don't have the cold heart to do what's needed. You're literally made of sunshine."

"Tell me!" Jasyn yelled, refusing to let Bron brush this off. For weeks, there had been so much secrecy and so many unanswered questions. Jasyn refused to be in the dark any longer.

"Execute the minister."

Jasyn stumbled backwards. "What?"

"My uncle is a monster worse than any dragon. He killed my mother, his *own* sister, because he wanted to avenge himself. Though," Bron tapped his chin, as if a thought just formed, "maybe your hatred of the minister would be enough to get you to act if you become king."

"I don't hate the minister," Jasyn said, but he had a feeling that was about to change.

"The minister stole your Iskra away from her home, like he does with all his dragons, and branded her as his property, cursing her to this doomed fate. She transforms each night and is locked in a cage, never able to stretch her wings. He's currently drugging her with a concoction of herbs to make her feral with the desire to kill." Bron pointed to the highest ledge, and Jasyn finally noticed the minister standing there. No wonder Iskra kept returning; she was getting another hit of the herbal smoke.

Jasyn felt his body go numb, and his eyes immediately stuck to Iskra, who continued her rotations around the cavern. He could tell she was getting hungrier for more action. He would need to start moving again soon.

"The minister hurt Iskra," Jasyn said. It was a plain statement, devoid of emotion, but deep inside, a well of anger was bubbling up toward the surface.

More words spilled from Bron, as if once he started, he couldn't stop himself. "I spent so much coin to try and save my mother. I am now in debt to the minister and need the wealth of being king to pay him back. The whole time, he knew it was his sister I was trying to keep alive, yet he leached everything from me, knowing he would never save her."

There was so much sadness and resentment in the way Bron spoke. It shattered something deep within Jasyn. While Jasyn could grieve his siblings' deaths without worry, Bron's own family member betrayed him.

"How much do you owe?"

Bron dipped his head, and there was so much shame in that small action. He didn't deserve to feel that way. Bron had been stuck in his own metaphorical cage for years, Jasyn realized. He saw this as the only way out—but it didn't have to be.

"We'll figure it out together," Jasyn offered. "But the only way I will ever dare help you is if Iskra comes out of this alive."

Bron took Jasyn in, contemplating whether to trust him. Jasyn hoped he would because he was being sincere.

"Then you better hold on tight," Bron said as he pushed Jasyn off the ledge.

Jasyn's eyes widened as he fell. He knew it wasn't far to the ground, but it could still kill him if he landed wrong.

He closed his eyes, preparing for all this to be over, but then, his body crashed into something else. Something that *moved*. Quickly, he held on to Iskra as she flew them both up.

Twenty

Jasyn squeezed his thighs tight as he situated himself. His sword was now long forgotten on the ground, and his hands had nothing to grip. If he wasn't careful, he would be another victim.

He gritted his teeth as Iskra swerved, and his body slid to the side. He expected her to do another loop around the cavern, but she seemed to slow her flight.

At first, he thought maybe Iskra didn't realize he was on her back. Then, he was being jerked around side to side as she landed on her perch.

He screamed as his body could no longer hold on, and he tumbled off her back onto the ledge with her. He hissed as rocks poked into him, his wounds agonizing, but the pain was barely noticeable as he scrambled away from her. He hit the cave wall, which wasn't far away at all. Her back was to him, but he had no doubt she sensed him there. She was thinking.

Jasyn peeked around him, searching for the Heart, and his own heart dropped to the pit of his stomach as no red glow surfaced. Was it on another ledge? But this was the one Iskra had been protective over this whole time. It must be here.

A chuckle sounded to his right, and Jasyn was greeted with the sight of Kryth waving the burning herbs near Iskra's snout. Jasyn was ready to pounce on the man, but the minister grabbed a rope and slid himself down easily. Jasyn's anger was so deep, he planned to follow Kryth down, but then he remembered who was actually important here.

Iskra's footsteps padded roughly across the ledge as she turned, and Jasyn leaned further into the wall, as if that would hide him better.

He prayed to Slone he would make it out alive, that he would leave victorious with the Heart in his hand—and more importantly, with Iskra in his arms.

This was the perfect moment to act, to do what he hoped would weaken but not kill her, but all thoughts were swept away as he saw it. Puncturing Iskra's chest, like a wound bleeding red, the ruby Heart of the Sun Court gleamed, taunting him. It was like a target, beckoning him forward. His breaths quickened as fear stormed his heart. Jasyn couldn't live in a world without Iskra. Just the thought had him keeling over.

Refusing to accept any other outcome but life, he squared his shoulders back and prepared for another way out. His first step was to get close to her.

"Iskra," he said, barely loud enough for his own ears, yet Iskra huffed through her nose.

He reached out his hand; she could come to him. He would show her he wasn't a threat. He loved her and wouldn't dare let any deathly harm come her away. She was his Sundrop, his blooming flower in the light.

His arm shook as she approached him, her steps loud as her tail swung. The rest of the cave didn't matter. It was just him and her.

"Iskra," he repeated.

She huffed again, but this time, it was more intense. The next few seconds were a quick blur. He saw her opening her mouth, and he dove right as fire blasted from her mouth. He was on his hands and knees, crawling away from the flame's path.

Getting away from her wrath must have angered her even more, because she let out another blast of fire. This time, he was trying to get up, which caused him to slow. Heat burned the back of his leg, and he choked down his scream. His legs wanted to buckle under the pain, but he leaned against the wall, keeping his body up.

Not for long, because Iskra was throwing more fire at him. Sweat coated almost every inch of his skin, his clothes clinging to him, as he ran along the wall, but he soon would be out of space.

He turned so his back was against the wall, and Iskra hadn't moved any further. She wouldn't need to take another step. Her stream of fire was long enough to cause damage even from that distance.

"My Iskra," he said. "I'm so sorry you have to do this."

Because he knew she hated it. If she had her own mind still, she would never attack him like this.

Another burst of his own anger hit him then. At the Gods and minister for letting a soul like Iskra be doomed to such a fate. At Iskra herself because of the lies and how she knew they were always on borrowed time. At himself for not worshipping Iskra more when they did have that time.

His life had unexpectedly led to this moment. He had lost and lost, and he refused to believe his destiny was to lose more, not after how much life Iskra had filled him with. Even his gardening didn't have the power to revive him like she did.

A whining noise came from Iskra, and Jasyn opened his eyes, scared someone was hurting her, only to realize she was in pain because of him.

Light poured from every inch of his body, beaming so brightly, his instinct was to squint—but he quickly realized the light didn't bother his eyes. It didn't hurt him at all. It had been years since his powers manifested like this, and if he wasn't currently threatened with dying, he would have cried tears of joy.

Iskra moaned, and he knew it was too much for her. She stumbled as she tried to look away, but it wouldn't protect her from how far his light reached. It was a flood of sunlight shining directly at her, and the consequences of staring at him would be detrimental, but he hoped at least it would not be deadly.

"Come here," he said quietly. Iskra needed to get close enough for him to rip the Heart from her chest.

But he knew she wouldn't approach him now, so he had to move. Jasyn walked slowly, hoping he was quiet enough for her not to hear him. He doubted that was the case. Her senses must be amplified in this form, but that also meant she was extra sensitive to the light. As long as he could keep it up, she would be distracted.

Her body heat strengthened as he reached her. It was overwhelming to be standing near something so much larger than him and willingly being here next to it. He took a breath to admire the enormity and strength of her. He couldn't believe this was the same person his heart had fallen for—even stranger was the desire for her after this was over, to want to ignore the arranged marriage with Esi and take Iskra's hand instead. He should condemn both of the women for lying to him, yet he couldn't.

Jasyn sighed, and perhaps it was the wrong thing to do, because his light extinguished, and before he had a chance to process, Iskra's tail swung under his feet, causing him to fall face-first. He grunted as his body hit cold rock, his knees sore from how he landed. Every inch of his skin felt like it was aflame, and the burn marks across his body seized at the impact.

He didn't allow himself to stop now. He got back up and faced Iskra, who had death in her eyes. He called to his light, and at first, the power didn't surface with the same brightness as before. He urged it on, thinking of his siblings who sacrificed themselves for the Undertaking, thinking of his father, who participated each year even with how dangerous it was. Finally, the light shined again.

Iskra whined as she directed her eyes away from him. This time, Jasyn ran.

He was at her in seconds, and her eyes couldn't take the light. She aimed her fire recklessly, and he had to dodge it. It didn't stop him from pushing onward. This would end now, with the Heart in his hands and Iskra alive.

Jasyn jumped over her flame, and as he did, he condensed his light to shine directly in her eyes. She bent her long neck backward, exposing her chest to him.

He took the small dagger he had sheathed at his thigh, wedged it underneath the Heart, and dug it out, a rush of her blood splattering his face. The ruby Heart of the Sun Court sprung across the ledge—right at Bron's feet.

Bron stared down at the Heart right below him. Jasyn expected him to lunge for it and claim victory, but he hesitated. His chest was heaving, like he'd climbed with speed to get here.

Iskra roared in pain. He hoped there was no permanent damage.

"I don't want this," Bron said, more to himself than Jasyn, but it was still loud enough for him to hear.

Jasyn slowly approached both Bron and the Heart, nervous if he moved too quickly, Bron would reconsider.

"You don't have to take it," Jasyn said. "We can find a way together to take down Kryth and get you out of debt."

Bron snapped his head up to Jasyn, and Jasyn feared he said the wrong thing until Bron's face crumpled.

"That won't bring her back."

"I know," Jasyn said, his voice soft. He sympathized with Bron. They both understood grief. "We will never be able to get the people we lost back. It's one of the hardest truths to ever accept—I'm not sure I ever will—but we persist for them, for a future they are not able to have."

Jasyn saw Bron wipe his nose, and Jasyn's own eyes burned. Yet, he couldn't have the comforting moment with the guard now. He had to act.

Jasyn bent down to grab the Heart, but before he could, he was being lifted off the ground, the blast of air from Iskra's wings causing Bron to stumble over.

She had him in her front talons.

"Don't touch the Heart!" Jasyn yelled as he was being carried away from the object that would finally end this.

He squirmed, but that only made Iskra tighten her hold.

"Iskra," he gritted through his teeth as he tried getting in a deep breath, but it was fruitless. Her hold squeezed tightly at his chest.

She was taking him higher and higher toward the skylight, as if she was planning to escape through the hole much too small for her large form. The height gave Jasyn a view of the whole cavern, Bron still on that ledge, now on his knees. He hadn't touched the Heart yet. Down below, he saw a moving form. Kryth was watching them, and even from this height, there was a satisfied glow radiating from the man.

There were a few other competitors scaling the walls. They would soon reach that ledge, and they would not hesitate to take the Heart. He had to get out of Iskra's hold and take it first.

His one arm, free from Iskra's grasp, banged against her talon in the hopes it would loosen her hold. It did for a short second, and he let out a deep breath, his chest filling with air.

He wished he was facing her. Maybe then, she would recognize who he was. But that was his hope persevering. Iskra did not remember him. If she did, she wouldn't be suffocating him.

With only one option he could think of, Jasyn lifted his hand and blasted light upward, praying it landed in her eyes again.

The groan that escaped her mouth told him he'd hit his mark. Perhaps too well, because he was slipping from her talons while they were still very high up.

Jasyn gripped her tightly so he wouldn't fall. Finally, he was at an angle where he could see Iskra. Her wings flapped, but they were still sinking downward. She just needed to bring them down a bit more, and Jasyn could attempt to leap onto the ledge with the Heart.

"Iskra," he whispered, not sure she could even hear his voice, unsure if he even wanted her to. Still, he had to get the words out. "I forgive you and Esi for tricking me. I understand now. You wanted freedom before doom, and you deserved that. I hope the time we had together brought you happiness. I hope I showed you how wonderful life was. Most importantly," he cleared his throat, "I hope you know I love you."

It was stupid to say these words when she didn't understand them, when his fate had been decided. He would marry Esi, like he promised his parents.

Yet, as Iskra struggled with his light, he dreamed of a life with her instead.

"I love you, Sundrop."

Those words must have woken something in her, because she stopped squirming. Her large eyes were directly on him, and he didn't shrink away from the scrutiny.

"I love you," he repeated.

Iskra groaned in pain, but the sound was less scary. There was regret in her eyes, but he shook his head, refusing to let that feeling overtake her.

He could feel they were flying downward.

Before he could question himself, he jumped from Iskra's arms and landed roughly on the ledge, where Bron knelt by the Heart, protecting it.

Jasyn ran and took it, ending the Undertaking while Iskra still lived. Yet, he didn't rejoice, because Iskra stopped flapping her wings, her body falling. Jasyn yelled out for her, knowing it was in vain. He crawled towards the ledge as she tumbled to the ground.

"No," Jasyn whispered, his eyes stinging with tears. He leaped over to grab the rope, but Bron stopped him.

"Wait." Jasyn fought back, but Bron's hold on him was tight. "Look."

Jasyn followed Bron's gaze to where Iskra began moving. Jasyn thought then that perhaps the gods didn't show Kryth everything, because as Iskra ripped his head off, that smile from earlier was gone.

Twenty-One

Back on the ground, Jasyn barely basked in the glory before he was sliding on his knees to Iskra in her human form. She was bare, and he hugged her tightly, feeling her shivering. All that fire must have blanked out of her the instant she had killed Kryth.

"Iskra, my Sundrop," he whispered as he stroked her auburn hair. Her real hair. He brushed the tangles out, begging for her to wake up.

This couldn't be the end for them both. He had too much to tell her.

Bron knelt beside him, taking her wrist in his hand. Jasyn wanted to yank it away from him, but Jasyn saw how he was applying pressure.

"There's a pulse," Bron said.

Jasyn didn't realize how much he needed that reassurance, because he shattered. His body shook as he tightened his hold on Iskra, never wanting to let her go.

Iskra woke up surrounded by warmth. A part of her thought she was returned to Slone, but her body felt too real, too mundane, to be with the Gods.

Her head pounded as she tried sitting up, but it was like she was tied down.

"I told Jasyn he tucked you in too tight," a familiar female voice said.

Swaths of dark hair appeared in Iskra's vision, and it was *almost* like looking in a mirror. She realized then that everything seemed muted around her, like everything was washed in a hazy gray. She went to touch her eyes, but they were obstructed by a pair of eyeglasses. Her brows scrunched, but she ignored that for now, focusing on the person in the room.

"Esi..." Iskra's voice was hoarse, her throat inflamed. She coughed, but that only made it hurt more, and Esi huffed.

"That's what you get for being a dragon."

Iskra ignored the jibe. "What happened?"

"Jasyn decided to bend the rules. He refused to kill you."

"The Heart?"

"Is his," Esi responded and crossed her arms. "With a little help from Bron along the way."

Flashes of the Undertaking came back to her, but it was still a blur. She doubted it would ever clearly come back to her, not with the herbal drugs Kryth had pumped into her.

"Why was Bron there?" Iskra felt she already knew the answer.

Esi sighed. "His history with the minister runs deep, and he felt like the only way out of his situation was becoming king and inheriting the royals' wealth."

Iskra blinked rapidly, letting the words sink in. It made sense why Bron chose to enter. He had been no way out of his dire situation with his uncle, but it still left a shooting ache in her chest to think of Bron competing against Jasyn.

Iskra's heart raced as she asked a question she had been dreading. "When are you and Jasyn going to be wed?"

Esi didn't say anything at first, wringing her hands together. That was when Iskra noticed her fingers were empty.

"We are not," Esi finally replied.

Iskra shook her head, unable to comprehend her words. "What do you mean you are not? That was the whole plan."

"Jasyn and I decided to forego the arrangement, to follow our hearts instead."

"Meaning?" Iskra pushed, and she didn't care how harsh it sounded.

Esi sat on the bed with Iskra. "Meaning I will marry Dominik, even if my parents disown me."

"Jasyn?"

"It's not my place to say."

Iskra nodded, frustrated to not get answers but also understanding. Then, Iskra asked the second question she had been dreading. "What has Kryzh said?"

Esi eyed her. "Do you truly not remember?"

Iskra shook her head, trying to think back, but it was still too fuzzy.

"You killed him."

Iskra blinked, not believing the words. Kryth couldn't be dead. Could he?

"I told you to get me as soon as she woke up," Jasyn snapped as he entered the room.

Iskra's heart stopped and restarted at the sight of him.

"You don't own her," Esi said, but her voice was lighthearted. "I wanted to speak with her, too."

Jasyn stilled but bowed his head. "Of course. Thank you for making sure she didn't awaken alone."

Esi pointed at Jasyn. "That's the respect I deserve."

Then, she was out the door with a quick wink at him.

Iskra tried fixing her hair slyly—she had no doubt it was a tangled mess—but Jasyn immediately clocked her movements. He shook his head, and she anticipated disapproval and anger, but instead, a soft smile lit his face.

"The color suits you," he said.

Iskra dipped her head in shame. "I'm so sorry for lying."

Jasyn put his hands out, and she immediately silenced herself.

"I've already spoken with Esi. She explained everything, and..." Iskra worried her bottom lip. "I understand why."

Iskra released a deep breath.

Jasyn kept talking. "I understand why you two decided to switch lives. Esi deserved that time with Dominik. You deserved freedom."

"It shouldn't have come at your expense," Iskra said.

"Reflecting on the whole situation now, it's a blessing."

Iskra scrunched her brows, but it caused a headache, so she relaxed her face again. "In what way?"

Jasyn sighed as he sat on the edge of the bed. The mattress dipped from his weight, and Iskra suddenly had the urge to tug him to her, to wrap her arms around his body.

"Esi loves Dominik. There's no changing that. If we married, she would be miserable, and I don't want a loveless marriage."

"So..."

"So she should marry Dominik. She has the future king's blessing. That should appease her parents."

The words hit her: Jasyn would soon be king. He fought and almost died, but he came out of the Undertaking alive, the Heart in his hand. He did it. Pride swelled in her chest.

"And you? What do your parents think about ending the engagement?"

Jasyn shrugged. "I think they're just relieved their final child is still alive."

"It must help that you won the Heart."

He nodded, and both were silent after that. Iskra let herself assess Jasyn. He had a large bruise along his cheek, and she instinctively reached out at the bandages on his neck. She wondered how many injuries she was directly responsible for.

"Don't blame yourself."

Iskra snapped her attention to Jasyn's face. "I hurt you," Iskra said plainly.

"I think you saved me," Jasyn responded. "I read your letter."

Iskra's face heated. "I know it was inappropriate for me to write that, especially given the circumstances.

"I'm glad I came out of the Undertaking alive to read it."

"Oh?"

"I don't know if you remember anything from the Undertaking, but I love you, Iskra. I've loved you for a long time now, but I was scared to admit it, especially since I was falling for someone different than I thought. It terrified me when I learned you weren't Esi, because that meant I wouldn't be marrying the person who made my heart glow."

As if on command, his body burst with light. Iskra looked through her tinted eyeglasses in adoration before she had to quickly turn away from the light, her eyes watering.

"You showed me what kind of king I could be, how my version of leading may be different but just as worthy. You showed me how to appreciate living again."

Iskra felt a hot tear run down her cheek. Jasyn was there, wiping it with his thumb, and then he was leaning his forehead against hers. She shut her eyes with how overwhelmed she was.

"I love you too," she whispered.

She felt him shudder, and she finally wrapped her arms around him. He fell on top of her, but she didn't care. The weight of him was comforting. He adjusted himself and climbed under the silk sheets with her, trailing his finger along her shoulder. "How do your eyes feel?"

Iskra blinked, a bit shocked by the question, but then she remembered the new addition to her face. She took the eyeglasses off and immediately regretted it. She squinted as she put them back on.

"I'm sorry," Jasyn said. "I blasted light directly in your eyes, and I think that may have impacted your vision. Looks like there is some sensitivity, like we guessed."

"I must look ridiculous." She pouted.

"You're still as beautiful as the sun."

"I thought I was prettier than the sun."

Jasyn snorted, and then a wild laugh escaped his lips, and Iskra laughed, too. It was an adjustment, no doubt, but...

"I'm alive because of you. I get to keep living, perhaps see more of the continent, because of you. I can live with having to wear these."

Jasyn smiled, but it didn't fill his face this time. "I think it's only in the daytime. We'll eventually tint the glass of the castle so you can walk around without them."

Iskra's face slackened. "You don't have to do that. I'll get out of your way, especially with your coronation coming up."

Jasyn pulled her in, and she fit perfectly against him. "You're not leaving me, Sundrop. Wherever you go, I follow."

"But—"

"Shh. Right now, you need rest, and this bed is too comfortable not to take advantage."

Iskra snorted, but he was right. Her body was tired.

"It'll be night soon."

"You haven't shifted since the Undertaking," Jasyn mumbled into her skin.

Her heart deflated at the words for some reason. Being a dragon had been a curse under Kryth's ownership. But now? It would have been a dream to be able to shift without that cage in her way, though she wondered how her eyes would be in that form.

"When you're better, we'll go out into a secluded field to test your powers. I have a feeling that since Kryth is dead, you'll be able to shift freely again."

Iskra could cry again. Jasyn wasn't afraid of her powers and understood they were special to her. Her heart didn't know if she could love him more.

Perhaps her love for him was like a plant. As each day a new branch sprouted, her love for him would grow.

Epilogue

Brimming with anticipated excitement, Jasyn led Iskra through a canopy of foliage.

"Slow down," Iskra hissed behind him. "My legs can't keep up with yours."

Jasyn did as she bade and stopped in his tracks. He pushed Iskra's tinted eyeglasses up her nose so they were straight. Then, he bent down and pressed a soft kiss to the tip of her nose.

She swatted him away. "Don't get too close, or you'll fog them up. It's already exhausting keeping these clean. Apparently, being free from Kryth did not free me from the mundane torture of cleaning glass."

Jasyn snorted. "Yet, you look more radiant than the sun."

Iskra rolled her eyes, but he meant it. Ever since she was able to get back on her feet, Iskra glowed. It was like she had swallowed some of his power during the Undertaking. Beneath the surface of her skin beat the faintest echo of his light, and right now, before first dawn, it became more prominent.

"As much as I want to admire you right here, we must keep moving."

"Why are we in a rush?" She pouted. Their days had been long, between meetings preparing for his coronation in two days' time, finally meeting Dominik for the first time, and finding a new minister.

Dominik had been lovely and cheery, a perfect fit for Esi. They would be leaving after Jasyn was crowned for the outskirts of the court, somewhere private, without any pressure on their relationship. Bron would not be joining the lady; he would be staying here, as a new member of the royal guard, working under Mych's command. Jasyn had no doubt Mych was delighted at the prospect of bossing Bron around. At first, Jasyn worried Mych wouldn't forgive Bron, but after some explaining, Mych had warmed up to him again. Now, they were inseparable, and Jasyn noticed how much lighter Bron walked with Kryth dead and his debts eliminated.

"Trust me and you'll learn," Jasyn replied to Iskra, who still didn't seem impressed.

He took her hand in his, and he savored how she clasped around him. They were like a lock and key, and he was forever grateful she was here with him still. It made letting go of her difficult, but he refused to cage her. Every day, she explored the town with less weight on her shoulders, and it was an honor to watch her live her new life. Most importantly, with practice, she had been able to shift on command again.

"As long as you promise to reward me after?" Iskra winked.

"I promise," Jasyn replied. Though she definitely spoke about a tumble in the sheets, there would be another reward waiting for her too.

If they got there.

"You're dragging your feet still," Jasyn noted, having to pull on her to keep a steady pace.

"Because I would rather be asleep next to you."

"Let's go, Sundrop," he said, this time bending down and lifting her.

She screeched with laughter and wrapped her arms around his neck. "You fell for my plan."

"Oh?" He raised a brow.

She wiggled her feet. "I knew you wouldn't be able to resist making sure I was comfortable."

He shook his head in amusement. How did he get so lucky to find someone like her? The woman in his arms would make sure he was never bored, never afraid to live the way he wanted.

"You're lucky we're almost there."

She nuzzled her head into his neck and pressed a gentle kiss to his skin. Goosebumps freckled across his flesh at her touch. He would never get used to it, the love in his heart that had blossomed.

They walked the rest of the way in silence. He suspected Iskra fell asleep, but he couldn't care less. She deserved to be well rested for this moment anyways.

As they neared their destination, Jasyn quietly nudged her awake. She made the smallest grunting noises as her eyes opened.

"We're here," he whispered, gesturing toward a gate so covered in vines, one couldn't see the other side. They were almost an hour's trek away from the castle, in a part of the court where nature roamed free.

"This better be good," she muttered as she got on her feet, facing him with tired eyes.

Jasyn took one last, deep breath before pulling open the door to let Iskra through, and the way her face lit up would be stamped into his memory for the rest of his life.

She was blinking furiously, but she wasn't able to stop the tears rolling down her face.

From her reaction, they got here at the perfect time. The sun just reached above the horizon, the field of sundrops opening in front of their eyes.

"It's beautiful," she said, so quietly, he barely heard it.

Jasyn joined her in the sundrop field, taking her hand again to encourage her forward.

"How is this here?"

Jasyn smiled. "It's always been here. I discovered it when I was young, and when I told my parents, they said it was here even before them, a gift from Slone or something."

"It's magical."

"I have so many good memories with my family here. And..." He cleared his throat, fully facing Iskra and taking both of her hands. "I want to add another."

Her eyes were wide in anticipation. Her cheeks were still tear-streaked, and she was the most magical thing in existence.

He realized then that this moment was inevitable. There would have been nothing and no one who could have stopped the two of them from reaching this point, holding hands in a field of sundrops with the waking sun above them.

"Iskra, you dug me out of the dark. You reminded me how full life can be as long as I wasn't afraid to live it. You gave me confidence to believe I could rule."

"It was always in you," she said, downplaying her magnificence. It would be his honor to ensure she was reminded of it each day—at least, if everything went how he hoped.

"Yet, there is one missing piece left to complete it all."

Her eyes were wide and unsure through those tinted glasses, so he reached into his pocket, took out the small box, and got on one knee. Iskra gasped, her hands covering her face.

"I need my Sundrop, my love, my queen, beside me. Will you marry me, Iskra?"

As the sun rose and the sundrops bloomed, Iskra laughed with tears in her eyes. She responded so brightly, it could be heard across the continent.

"Yes!"

Acknowledgements

After two years of ideating and writing and publishing, it's officially the end of The Weather Court Gem series. It's such an emotional goodbye for me. I have spent so much of my time thinking about this world and all its characters, and now, the world gets to experience them all.

I put so many hours into each of these novellas, but I had the help of amazing people along the way.

Aubrey: It has truly been an honor to work together on these covers. You have created such masterpieces that I am so obsessed with.

Alexis: Thank you for stepping in and editing this final novella.

Des: Your beta reading and editing throughout this whole series is so appreciated. You have truly made all these stories so much stronger because of your feedback.

Finally, readers, I thank you for stepping into this world with me. I hope you enjoyed these stories of love as much as I had writing them.

About the Author

KC Silver is a born and raised Chicagoan who just moved to NYC, where she spends her days exploring the city, one train stop at a time with a sweet treat in hand. She currently works in advertising where she daydreams of the day when a Slack notification no longer makes her heart jump in fear.

KC enjoys character driven stories where the main character is on a journey of discovering themselves and learning to let go of the expectations weighing on them, while falling in love.

She can be found on all socials @bysilverstories

www.ingramcontent.com/pod-product-compliance
Lightning Source LLC
LaVergne TN
LVHW041944070526
838199LV00051BA/2902